My Brother's Keeper 3

Love, Lies & Betrayal

Tina J

Copyright 2020

More Books by Tina J

A Thin Line Between Me & My Thug 1-2
I Got Luv for My Shawty 1-2
Kharis and Caleb: A Different kind of Love 1-2
Loving You is a Battle 1-3
Violet and the Connect 1-3
You Complete Me
Love Will Lead You Back
This Thing Called Love
Are We in This Together 1-3
Shawty Down to Ride For a Boss 1-3
When a Boss Falls in Love 1-3
Let Me Be The One 1-2
We Got That Forever Love
Ain't No Savage Like The One I got 1-2
A Queen & Hustla 1-3 (collab)
Thirsty for a Bad Boy 1-2
Hasaan and Serena: An Unforgettable Love 1-2
We Both End Up With Scars
Caught up Luvin a beast 1-3
A Street King & his Shawty 1-2
I Fell for the Wrong Bad Boy 1-2 (collab)
Addicted to Loving a Boss 1-3
All Eyes on the Crown 1-3
I Need that Gangsta Love 1-2 (collab)
Still Luvin' a Beast 1-2
Creepin' With The Plug 1-2
I Wanna Love You 1-2
Her Man, His Savage 1-2
When She's Bad, I'm Badder 1-3
Marco & Rakia 1-3
Feenin' for a Real One 1-3
A Kingpin's Dynasty 1-3
What Kind Of Love Is This?
Frankie & Lexi 1-3
A Dope Boy's Seduction 1-3
My Brother's Keeper 1-3

Previously…

Dashier

"Did Mari get in yet?" I asked Genesis the fifth time this morning.

"No, she said her doctor's appointment was today. Did you forget?" She told me in the phone and I relaxed a little.

The two of us spoke last night and Jose told me he made her an appointment because she was taking too long and his kid needed vitamins. Mari refused to entertain the thought of being pregnant but he was adamant she is carrying his child. I agreed with him making her an appointment because she wouldn't have.

"I did forget. Do you know what time it was?" She hung the phone up and knocked on the open door to my office.

"Are you ok? Is there something wrong with Mari?"

"Nah, it's just not like her to go this long without calling."

"Maybe they're celebrating, like we should be." I looked up at her.

"What we celebrating?"

"That you admitted to being in love with me." She straddled my lap and my dick woke right up for her.

"What did I tell you about office sex?"

"You promised to make love to me here under the city lights too. Just because you told me at home doesn't mean I don't still wanna do it."

"Whenever you're ready."

"I'm always ready for this." She undid my pants, pushed my chair back and got on her knees.

"Got damn baby." Her mouth was soaking wet and she was swallowing my dick whole.

"Mr. Davis, there's someone downstairs requesting to see you." Maxine said when she came in. I thought Genesis would stop.

"Ok. Fuck!" Genesis had my balls juggling in her mouth. She knew I loved that shit.

"Is everything ok?"

"Yea, I'm just thinking about something. Got dammit."

"You sure, you're ok?" She asked again.

6

"I'm fine. Do me a favor and close the door on the way out and whoever is downstairs let them know, I'll be there in a few minutes. Oh shit." Maxine gave me a crazy look. I waved her off and hurried her to close the door. My nut was at the tip and if she didn't leave, I can't say she wouldn't have figured it out.

"Let it go Dash." She whispered and winked.

"Shitttttttttt. Genesis, fuck." I gave her a lot and watched as she suctioned it all out and wiped her mouth with the back of her hand.

"Stay right here." I went over to the door, locked it, took my shirt off and placed her on all fours on my desk.

"You wanna play right? You better not make one fucking sound and I mean it." I spread her ass cheeks and dove right in, taking turns licking and sucking on her pussy and ass.

"Dashhhhh." She whispered silently. I let my pants and boxers fall to my ankles as she succumbed to that orgasm.

"You better not get loud or I'm gonna fuck you real hard." She nodded and bit down on her arm when I sat her on my dick, cowgirl style. Her head was lying on my chest as I fucked her from the bottom.

"Fuck me back Genesis." She placed her hands on my legs and popped her pussy the way I liked it.

"Yea ma. This pussy talking to me." She bent over further and I stood to hit it from the back.

"No noise." She nodded her head and I could tell she was struggling to keep the moans in, the same way I was.

"Oh shit Dash, I'm about to cum again and…"

"And what?" I watched her body shake and juices spit out.

"I love you Genesis." I held her tight and for the first time, released my seeds in a woman since my ex. My siblings are having kids so I may as well join them. I lifted her up and sat her on my lap. She was exhausted and snuggled her face in my neck.

"I love you too baby." She put her legs on my lap.

"Mr. Davis, the person downstairs is being rude and requesting your presence right away." Maxine spoke though the intercom.

"Call my friends at the precinct and have two of them stop by. I'll be right down." I'm no punk but when someone comes into a bank requesting to see the CFO, its usually to rob them or some other shit.

"Everything ok?" I walked in the bathroom with Genesis and we cleaned ourselves up.

"Yea, it should be. When I leave, wait a few minutes and come out. Maxine will be with me but until the elevator arrives, she'll be stalking my office door."

"Stalking is all she better do."

"It is sexy. I'll see you in a few." I kissed her lips and closed the door behind me.

"Let's go Maxine." I checked for my weapon and pressed the elevator button. I noticed my sister door was closed.

"Did my sister walk past you?"

"No, maybe her secretary is in there." I smirked because it meant she had no idea someone was with me.

"Oh ok. I'll check when we're done with whoever this is." We stepped on the elevator and she hit the lobby button.

Once the doors opened, I sucked my teeth. Why is this bitch even here?

"Hello Dashier. This is my lawyer, Mr. Collins and I think you know who this is." The guy turned around and I could've beat that smirk right off his face.

"A lawyer for what Nika?"

"My son. You know the one I can't see because you keep him away?" Before I got to speak, I heard Genesis calling me in a distressed tone. I noticed a phone in her hand and a sad look on her face. Something told me it was about my sister but I had to wait for her to speak.

"What's wrong?" I asked and she froze.

"Hello Genesis."

"What… what are you doing here?" Her body started shaking.

"Oh, I was just about to inform Mr. Davis here, how you are going to be arrested for planning to rob this bank." Two officers came through the door.

"SAY WHAT?" I shouted and turned to look at her.

"Oh, Genesis here is just like her cousin. Ain't that right?" Genesis stood there stuck and my gun went straight to her forehead.

"Tell me right now Genesis if you were using me and planning on robbing my bank." I cocked my gun and waited for her answer. When she remained silent, it was Nika all over again.

"Dash." She had tears running down her face. There's no way this could be happening to me again. Does God really hate me that much?

Demaris

"You got one more time to fight with my baby in your stomach." Jose said in a firm and strict tone. He finally took me outta time out after seducing him in the office. I know he wanted to leave me in it longer but it never works out the way he wants. I did miss him and made sure to show him my appreciation.

"We don't even know if I am."

"Lucky for you, we're about to find out." He gave me a smile. I knew he wanted a baby and I probably am pregnant but I won't tell him because his arrogant ass, got on my nerves.

He parked in front of the doctor's office and we both stepped out. My bladder was about to bust if I didn't hurry up and use the bathroom. He opened the door for me and smiled as I signed in. The two of us found seats and instead of sitting in a chair, he sat me on his lap and kissed me.

I was so in love with this man and I hope he doesn't leave me if I am pregnant. Too many men are happy in the beginning and bounce before or after the baby is born. You know they make the perfect promises and disappear when you least expect it.

"I'm not gonna leave you Mari."

"You better not." He rubbed my belly and kissed it. Some woman sitting across from us smiled and laid her head on the guy's shoulder next to her. It is nice to see people in love, which is why I'm so happy Genesis is in Dash's life. It took him a long time to find love after Nika, but it's been worth the wait let him tell it.

"Ms. Davis." The nurse called me and walked us to the back.

"Hey Jose." I turned to see the thirsty bitch of an ex.

"Don't you move." He pushed me in the room and made me do what the nurse asked. I peed in the cup and got undressed.

"Why is she here?"

"Hell if I know. Open those legs real quick so I can shine the light and see what the doctors see." And like the freak I am for him, I did it.

"It looks fat and juicy Mari." I shook my head laughing.

13

"If she is, it's because you made her that way." He shut the light off and pressed his lips on mine.

"Damn right I did. You wanna cum for me." He moved the sheet and began circling my clit.

Knock! Knock! He stopped and told me he wanted to see it under the light again before leaving.

"Hello, Ms. Davis." The doctor introduced herself, told me I was expecting and put the gel on and let us see our baby. After asking a ton of questions, she stepped out and this nasty nigga locked the door, pulled a chair up and turned the light back on.

"Now let me see you cum under the light."

"Make me." He placed some kisses on my clit before taking me to ecstasy. When I was about to cum, he replaced his mouth with his fingers and watched my juice's squirt out.

"That shit sexy Mari. I'm gonna put a light on your pussy every time I eat it." He washed my pussy with a warm paper towel and helped me up.

"I wonder how that dick look cumming under the light." He grabbed himself and I unbuckled his jeans.

14

"Are you ok Ms. Davis?" The nurse knocked on the door.

"I'll be right out."

"I got you at home baby." He opened the door and this bitch was standing there.

"Are congratulations in order again?"

"Again?" I heard Jose suck his teeth.

"Oh Jose didn't tell you how I terminated our baby because he didn't want it." I swung my body around to look at him.

"Go head Dutchess."

"Oh, you didn't tell her. Well it's really a funny story. Demaris, is it?" She followed us out the door and into the parking lot. Jose gave me a look not to touch her.

"You see, he got me pregnant and was ecstatic about having a child and spending the rest of his life with me." I stopped walking, when I should've kept going. I know she was bitter and wanted him back which means she will say anything.

But why did she say inside he made her get rid of it for not wanting a child with her? Now she's saying something

15

else? However, he didn't object to any of the information she spoke of.

"We were gonna get married, raise our family and live happily ever after but guess what Demaris?"

"Get the fuck outta here." Jose was becoming angrier.

"He cheated on me." I gasped and covered my mouth in shock.

"Bye Dutchess." He always told me he wasn't a cheater but she's saying different.

"No, I think her hearing we almost shared a child and you telling her the same things you told me is enough to hurt her, don't you think." I had tears running down my face. Not because of him cheating but because she was right. Everything he told her, he told me.

"Were you tryna replace her by being with me?"

"WHAT? Mari, don't let her get in your head." He hit the alarm on the truck and told me to get in.

"Jose did you say those things to her?"

"Let's go Mari."

"I know you were in love with her at one time and I can expect some of the words to be similar. But it's like you repeated the same thing to me."

"And me." I turned to see Talia standing there with a grin on her face.

"No, no, no. Not again. Jose, please tell me they're lying." I felt my body getting weaker as he stood there tryna find the right words to say.

"Mari, let's talk about this at home."

"One more question Mari. Does he tell you how warm, tight and how you have the best pussy ever? I mean his words can definitely hypnotize a bitch." I saw Jose walking towards Talia and her body hit the ground. He turned to Dutchess and before he could swing off, cops pulled up.

"GET ON THE GROUND." One cop yelled at Jose, hopped out the car and shielded his body with the car door. I instantly became nervous for him.

"Hell no!"

"SIR, I'M GONNA TELL YOU ONE MORE TIME TO GET ON THE GROUND!" The cop looked scared to death, which means this is about to go left.

"Jose, do what he says." He paid me no mind and gave Dutchess a hateful stare. I had no doubt in my mind that he's gonna kill her.

"Stop this Dutchess. You're a cop. Please tell them to leave him alone." She had a smile on her face.

"GET DOWN NOW!" Another officer came up with his gun pointed at him.

"Jose, please get down."

"Mari, I ain't do shit. Talia deserved that punch and if these cops weren't here, I'd knock her the fuck out too."

"I know. Just do what they say." He started to come to me.

"Mari, don't believe shit they say."

"Ok baby, I don't. Please stop and get down." I was hysterical crying and out the corner of my eye, saw Dutchess speaking to an officer. Once he nodded, I knew this would be it.

18

"He should've gave me another chance." She whispered in my ear. Jose went to grab my hand and shit went terribly wrong.

"HE HAS A GUN!" Dutchess yelled out and it was like my life flashed in front of me. Shots were fired and everything else was a blur.

Dashier

"I'm going to ask one more time. Were you using me and planning to rob my bank?" After hearing about the lawyer and Genesis, I moved us into one of the small rooms because customers and workers continued staring. I closed the door and witnessed the tears making Genesis vison even more blurry. She used the back of her hands to wipe them. What was she crying for?

"Who the fuck cares at this point? My son is going home with me and…" I backhanded the shit outta Nika, forgetting about Genesis at the moment. It wasn't that I didn't care but my son came before her and if this bitch thought for a second she was taking him, she had another thing coming.

"Did you see that Mr. Collins?" She asked tryna remove herself from Manny's grip. He's the one who caught her just as she was about to fall. Not only was she tryna take my son, my heart was broken again by a woman claiming to love me, yet; used me for the same shit my ex, her cousin did.

"Maybe we should talk about this later." Her lawyer requested and I shut it down. I moved in his space and noticed

20

he sweat beads coming down his forehead. Now he wants to discuss this later after the spectacle they caused. Nah, we about to deal with this shit right now.

"Mr. Collins, is it?" He nodded and swallowed hard.

"I'm not sure what she told you, nor do I care. What I do care about is a man with your stature coming into my place of business demanding to see me, and allowing your so-called client and her friend to make accusations about my staff."

"I'm… I'm…" He tried to apologized as I fixed the tie on his now sweaty shirt.

"No need to apologize because see I know the type of woman Shanika is. I can guarantee, she sold you a dream about getting paid when she attempts to seek custody of my son, which we both know she won't get."

"Yes I will. You're fucking my cousin who is tryna bring you down and do exactly what I did?" I turned to see Maxine staring at Genesis, who was trying to get away from Manny.

"Making false accusations about who I'm sleeping with is unnecessary and so is all this drama you brought. Officers

21

please escort them out and if you allow either one of them back in, you will be terminated." I told the security guards who had nervous looks on their faces. I made my way over to where Genesis was and overheard him speaking to her.

"You think that nigga wants you? He looks at you like a ho and you know why? Because you slept with your cousins ex. Regardless; of what they went through only ho's do shit like that."

"Manny, just go."

"I'm not leaving my woman with that maniac. Do you have any idea what he's gonna do when we leave? Nika already told me how crazy he is and if you don't come with me, there's no telling if you'll live to see another day."

"Excuse me. Genesis you can go upstairs to retrieve your things." Maxine said and I thought Genesis was gonna beat her ass.

"She's right. A lot has taken place, things were said and unless you work as a teller, I'm going to have everyone take the rest of the day off." She went to walk off and he gripped her arm.

"The only way she's going up there, is if I'm going with her." I elbowed the shit outta him in the face.

"I don't know what type of shit people allow you to do in Alabama, but putting your hands on a woman ain't what we do here."

"Says the man who just hit his baby mama." I chuckled.

"I'll knock anyone the fuck out if they're tryna take my kid." He didn't say anything.

"Now like I said, she can go retrieve her things and take the day off. If she wants to leave with you, then that's on her." I nodded and security held him back as the three of us stepped on the elevator.

I kept my head in the air watching the numbers light up to the third floor. Once they stopped, I stepped off and made a beeline to my office. Something told me Maxine would follow and sure enough, when I turned around there she stood.

I can admit Maxine is a very pretty white woman, but she portrays herself to be better than all my staff. It's no secret she wants me to fuck her, however; employee or not, I'd never stick my dick in her. Then, she wears these ugly ass hair

23

weaves for some reason. I mean the hair goes down to her ass at times. The women make fun of her but she swears by her appearance.

"Do you need me in here while you terminate her?" I ignore her, poured myself a shot and continued staring out the window."

"Mr. Davis, do you...?"

"Close my door on the way out Maxine." I never turned around and listened to the door shut. Not even two minutes later there was a knock. I let the shot burn my chest and sat the glass on the desk.

"Come in." I removed my tie and placed the jacket on the back of my chair.

"Can we talk?" I let out a laugh.

"Talk about what Genesis? How you possibly betrayed me the same way your cousin did? And I say possibly because she's a got damn liar too. Or the fact your man showed up here believing you two are still a couple?" I was livid when he said they were still together because it meant she never broke up

24

with him. I guess she assumed staying in Jersey should make him think it.

"Dashier, I…" I put my hand up and made my way to her. I let my hand slide in that pretty hair of hers I loved and stared in her eyes. I could see she had some feelings for me but with the shit her cousin and man said, I didn't know who to believe.

"I would've given you the world if you asked for it Genesis."

"I didn't.-"

"Shhhhh." I pecked her lips.

"I'm having a hard time dealing with this and you of all people should know how I feel when someone betrays me." She let tears drain out her eyes again.

"I love you Genesis and possibly put my child in you, but right now I can't stand the sight of you and its best for you to leave."

"I love you too Dash and I want this child if you did get me pregnant." I let her go.

"Each second that passes, I see betrayal, lies and most of deceit." I grabbed my phone and keys.

"If you happen to pop up pregnant, get rid of it. Matter of fact, here's $100 to pick up a Plan B pill. I refuse to have a child with another bitch who can try and take me for all I got."

"Bitch?" She wiped her eyes and came to me.

"That's what I said."

"You know Dash, I wanted to explain what happened downstairs but you see what you want and I understand, but don't call me out my name."

"I'm a grown ass man and say what the fuck I want." My temper was rising.

"You're right but Dashier, I'm the woman you fell in love with. The one who's helping you raise Kingston and the one you love."

"Nah, the woman I loved would've never kept a man waiting in the wind thinking they were still a couple. The woman I loved, would've never allowed them to make me believe you could possibly be tryna steal from me. The woman I loved, would've opened her mouth downstairs and made sure

I knew what they said was a lie. This woman in front of me is a fraud."

"Dashier, please."

"I'm done with you Genesis."

"No you're not because I'm not done with you." She ran over to me at the door and placed both hands on the side of my face.

"Dash, please don't leave me. I love you and if you need me to set them up on video and record the fact they were lying, I would. Just please don't leave me." She was breaking my heart but I was still confused.

"The condo is in your name and so is the car. Your personal belongings will be delivered shortly so there's no need for you to drop by. You can keep your job here but do me a favor and stay on that side of the office. We have no affiliation with one another as of today." I opened the door and she fell on her knees crying harder.

"If you want to see Kingston, contact my sister and she'll drop him off. From this day forward, you are only an employee. You will address me as the boss and that's only if we need to speak. Any questions, go through my secretary and if you send me any, *I'm sorry, can we talk, or I miss and love you text,* I swear on my son, I will take everything you have and put your ass back on a plane to Alabama. Do I make myself clear?" She didn't respond. I went over, used my hand to tilt her face and made her look at me.

"Do I make myself clear?"

"Dash." She had snot and tears running down her beautiful face.

"DO I?" I shouted because it was killing me to see her this distraught but until I find out the truth, this is how it has to be.

"Yes." I snatched my hand away, stepped out my office and slammed the door. Glass shattered everywhere. I was so got damn mad that if I didn't leave now it's no telling what I would've done to her.

"Mr. Davis." I heard Maxine shout and turned to see her switching fast in my direction.

"What?"

"Your mother called. She's been trying to get in touch with you." I pressed the elevator button.

"Did she say what she wanted?" She gave me a somber look.

"She said you need to get to the hospital. Your sister needs you." Instead of waiting on the elevator, I took the stairs and hauled ass down them. I left out the side door and this punk ass nigga was still here.

"Didn't I tell your stupid ass to leave?" He looked me up and down and scoffed up a laugh.

"I'm waiting on my girl."

"Well wait for her down the street." He sucked his teeth.

"Nigga, don't make me do you like I did in Alabama." He strolled off but not without saying something.

"Genesis got some banging ass pussy, don't she?"

"What nigga?"

"That's why you're mad. You don't want her sharing it with no one. Welcome to my world." He hit me with a peace sign and kept it moving.

I may not want to admit it but he was right. I didn't wanna be without her but at this moment we need to be apart. Of course, I don't want another nigga fucking her. However; if she finds someone else in the process, so be it. I'm not gonna let it bother me now. My sister needs me.

Genesis

I held my knees to my chest and continued rocking back and forth. It's been a half hour and I hadn't moved from the spot Dashier left me in. Not only was I distraught he left but angry at my cousin and Manny for stooping so low to hurt me. I wasn't bothering either of them and couldn't understand for the life of me, why they did this. I do know I'm going to find out.

I finally found the strength to stand, fixed my clothes and went in his bathroom to clean up. Looking in the mirror, I saw the eyeliner and mascara smeared on my face, as well as nasty ass dried up snot, clinging from pieces of my hair onto my face. It's quite disgusting and I see why Dash had to leave. I probably turned his stomach. I wet some paper towels and began scrubbing.

When I finished a smile graced my face reminiscing about the things he and I did in here about an hour ago. Then, a frown formed knowing we'd never be together again. I saw the love in his eyes and confusion. He had every right to be in his feelings after hearing the things they accused me of. But if he gave me a chance to explain, he'd know it was all a lie.

I'd never rob a bank, especially; not his. I'm scared of jail and no amount of fake promises from anyone could make me do it. People do crazy things in love but I'm not doing shit to make me get three meals a day and lose my freedom.

I stepped out his office and walked with my head held high to my desk on the other side. It's not far but you can't see his office from where my desk sat. I saw the women staring at me, yet; no one said a word. Either they were scared I'd tell Demaris or worried Dashier would return and catch them. It didn't bother me because I'm used to hating ass chicks talking shit. To me, it's just another day in the life of Genesis Tyler.

Yes, I used my father's name Rogers for all personal information and in case if emergency. I only used my mom's maiden name if I didn't want anyone to find me. I guess it don't matter which one I used because my ex found me. I guess he would hanging with my hateful cousin. And before anyone asks, no he didn't know my other name. He met me as Genesis Rogers so what's the need to mention it.

32

Ok, so I didn't verbally break up with Manny but he should've known. I never answered his calls and changed my number. He was blocked from my social media accounts and I called the landlord to my old place and told him, I no longer stayed there. Manny wasn't on the lease so he most likely kicked him out. Once I didn't return it should've been a dead giveaway of us being over. Yet; here I am dealing with his stupid ass again.

"Mr. Davis asked for your ID card." Maxine stood there with her arms folded.

"Try again. He told me to take the remainder of the day off, like he told everyone else. Trust that I'll be here tomorrow."

"Ms. Rogers." I slammed my stuff down.

"You're really testing my patience bitch and I'm trying my hardest not to mop this floor with your fake nappy weave wearing ass." Her white ass backed up.

"Yea you brought the ghettoness out and I hate to be the one to tell you this, but if I have to whoop your ass, you'll probably end up in the hospital."

"Is that a threat?"

"No ma'am. It's a fucking promise. Now try me." I waited for her to even flinch and I planned on beating the fuck outta her. My ass needed to get rid of this frustration too.

"Just go and leave your ghettoness as you call it, at home tomorrow." She swung her dirty blond hair and stormed off. I noticed a few women give me a thumbs up. I shook my head because someone should've put her in her place a long time ago.

I gathered the rest of my things, shut down the computer and clocked out. I saw others doing the same as I made my way to the elevator. Another woman pressed the button before me and we stepped on together with two others. At first, none of them said a word but one finally broke the ice.

"Thanks so much for doing that to Maxine."

"You're welcome but why haven't any of you done it?" I was curious because they were working here longer than me, which means they've been dealing with it for a while.

"The bitch always talking shit and then threatens to tell Mr. Davis some off the wall shit. If we request a meeting with

34

him, she's usually sitting in on them with her ugly ass." I busted out laughing.

"And you know all emails are screened by her first so we can't do that. None of us are privy to his personal number and HR don't wanna hear it. They be like, *well Mr. Davis had her for years and unless you have solid proof he won't believe you.*"

"She's not supposed to tell you that." I said a little angry when we stepped off and into the lobby. Business went back to normal and it didn't seem like anything took place here.

"We know but guess what?" I stopped and looked at them.

"The bitch in HR is her sister."

"Get the fuck outta here." I covered my mouth because I was a tad bit loud. I opened the door and we all stepped into the parking lot.

"What you about to do?" One of them asked. I still had no idea what their names were.

"Not a damn thing."

"Come out with us to Applebee's. It's happy hour and from the way you looked after coming out his office, you can use a drink."

"I look that bad?" They gave each other a look.

"Not anymore. But when you came from downstairs your ass was hit. Makeup a mess, all that." I laughed.

"Fine. I'll follow you. What's your name?"

"I'm Ashanti, that's Mira and she's Charlie."

"I'm Genesis."

"We know."

"And that means?"

"It means, Maxine has been whining about you since getting hired. We'll discuss it more over drinks." I hit the alarm on my car and almost broke down when I got in. Everything in here reminded me of Dash.

BEEP! BEEP! The horn took me outta the crying fit I almost had. Thank goodness because I refused to go for drinks with my face tore up.

****

"Where the fuck you been?" Manny snatched me out my car in front of the condo. I just got home from happy hour feeling great and he just ruined it.

"Get the fuck off me and how do you know where I stay?" He smirked and this bitch stepped out.

"I should've known."

"Yea, you should've." Nika swung missing me and I started tagging her ass.

I don't do the grabbing hair thing because I feel like it's cheating. How the person supposed to give you any competition if you swinging their head? To me it's a cop out and showing a bitch ain't really sure about her hands. Manny finally pulled me off her and her lip and eye was bleeding.

"You stupid bitch."

"I'll be stupid but I bet you won't get your son or the nigga." She thought what I said was hilarious.

"Yes I will dummy. You just proved he's not safe around the violent woman who raised him all these years." Now it was my turn.

"And you just proved you waited for me to come home, just to attack me." I pointed to the cameras outside the condo.

"Those shits don't even work." She spit on the ground next to my feet. I grabbed my phone out the car, shut the door and pulled up the app.

"What were you saying?" I showed the three of us standing at this exact moment.

"Whatever."

"Get in the house. Bye Nika." I walked to my door and unlocked it.

"Where are you going?" I asked Manny as Nika went to the car.

"With you. We together until the very end."

"Lies you tell." I pushed him back, ran in and slammed the door. I heard him cursing and yelling for me to let him in.

When I heard a loud crash, I peeked out the window and saw him literally jumping on the back of my windshield. He kicked the side windows out too.

I took my phone out and recorded everything he did at the same time I was calling 911 from the house phone. He's not about to get me put out or make Dash think I'm ruining his property. *Childish ass nigga.*

Demaris

"Get down baby." Jose refused to listen to me. When the two bullets ripped through his chest and he hit the ground, my vision became blurry. My mouth was screaming out no, but there was no sound. I don't know if the gunshots were too loud or what. All I know is when I saw him lying there and blood spilling out, I couldn't take it and started beating Dutchess ass. I wasn't worried about my child or going to jail, just getting her.

"Let her go ma'am." The guy pulled me off and ran over to check on her. I saw some nurses hovering over top of Jose and ran to him. I was on my knees, holding his hand and rubbing his head.

"Mari. Where's Mari." I heard him whisper.

"I'm right here baby. Don't leave me. Please don't leave me."

"Watch out everyone." Some guy moved me out the way. I looked and it was the Paramedics. They started working on him, placed him on the stretcher and in the back. You damn right I jumped in.

I watched my man die twice in front of me and almost caused an accident. When Jose flatlined, I started screaming and scared the driver. It wasn't done purposely but when the person you love literally leaves this earth and comes back, it's scary and amazing at the same time. It's like he wanted to be rid of the pain and God kept telling him no, it's not his turn and sent him back.

When they pulled up to the hospital, doctors and nurses were standing there waiting. They helped get the stretcher down and rushed him to the back. I was hysterical crying; my body was shaking and I could barely stand. I heard someone asking if I were ok and felt another person trying to sit me in a chair. It's like the moment my bottom half touched the chair I began feeling weaker.

The nurse said my adrenaline was no longer pumping and my body needed a break. She asked for my ID and I had none. The only person I could think to call was Dash. Genesis answered her cell and I waited for him to get on but he never did. I gave them Jose's full name and address and told them to contact his sister. I laid on the two chairs next to me and fell asleep.

****

"Wake up Mari." I heard Rakim's voice but it's no way he came. He shook me a little harder and I opened my eyes.

"Stop shaking her like that Rakim." Dash said.

"What the...?" I tried to lift my hand and it was handcuffed to the bed. Two officers were standing inside the room and so was Dutchess. She had the nerve to be talking to my parents. Did I miss something?

"Why the fuck are these cuffs on me and get her the fuck outta here." The monitors were beeping loudly and my heart felt as if it were racing.

"Mari, calm down."

"DON'T TELL ME TO CALM DOWN! SHE'S THE REASON JOSE IS HERE. OH MY GOD! WHERE IS HE? IS HE OK? DASH, PLEASE GO SEE IF HE'S OK." I started crying hysterical.

"Mari please relax and tell us what happened." My mother asked when she came closer. I noticed my father giving Dutchess the evil eye and Rakim gave me a death stare.

"I was at the doctors and she followed us."

"Why would she follow you?"

"Ma, you have no idea." I was still keeping my relationship quiet in front of Rakim and I don't know why.

"We were coming out and she started talking shit to me. Talia was with her and between the two of them, they began taunting me about Jose. Long story short, Jose was trying to tell me they were lying and this bitch whispered something in a cop's ear."

"What do you mean she whispered in his ear?" My father was confused and so was everyone else.

"I think she told the cop to shoot Jose?"

"How do you know?" Dash asked.

"Because she's a bitch."

"Mari that's not necessary." My mom said. I guess she didn't want me to be rude in front of the cops but fuck them.

43

"All I know is, she tells me Jose should've given her another chance and yelled out he had a gun. The cops shot him and I beat her ass. Ma, why did she do that?" They all glanced over by the door where she stood or should I say, did stand and her and the two officers were no longer there. Dash and Rakim ran out and came back to say she was nowhere in sight.

"What's going on Mari?" Rakim asked and since my parents, Dash and my two other brothers walked in, I felt like he couldn't touch me.

"Jose and I have been seeing each other for months now. I was at the doctors finding out if I were pregnant."

"Let me get this right." Rakim paced the small area of the room with his fist balled.

"I told you to leave that nigga alone because he was no good for you. You fuck with him anyway. His ex comes back and gets mad he no longer wants her. She follows y'all to the hospital and has him shot. And then you beat her up for getting him shot."

"Pretty much."

"Did it ever dawn on you that she's a GOT DAMN COP MARI? NOW YOU'RE ABOUT TO GO TO JAIL FOR A MAN WHO'S EX IS HELL BENT ON GETTING HIM BACK." He shouted and no one said a word.

"You kept all of it a secret from me and now look." He put his hands on top of his head.

"This is the exact reason I told you he was no good for you."

"Whatever?" Who is he to tell me who's good enough or not?

"I didn't know he had excess baggage but I knew he was a street nigga and with those type of men, a lotta problems come with them."

"You mean like how you're tryna hide the fact you're one of the biggest dope dealers in town." He stopped and stared at me.

"Yea, I know all about you and no he didn't tell me."

"Who told you that?" He had an evil look on his face.

"The night mommy told us about the family helping daddy over in Puerto Rico, I asked Jose if he ever heard of anyone by that name. Unbeknownst to him, he answered and gave me a rundown of how the family is huge and the empire is now run by their son MJ. Imagine my surprise when he mentioned him supplying most of the U.S.

I went by your office to speak with you about it and Ced let me in the office. Who knew you had all that info on your computer? You really should log out when you leave your office."

"Tha fuck Mari?"

"I saw pick up and drop off dates. You need a better system because you're gonna get caught." I shrugged my shoulders and rolled over.

"Listen here you spoiled bitch." He had me by my hair.

"WHOA!" Efrain, Dash and Levi pushed him back against the wall.

"So y'all ok with her fucking with a nigga who brought this drama to her front door?"

"Rakim Davis, you apologize to her right now." My mom shouted and he stared at me.

46

"Not this time ma. I love you but this is her shit and I'm not apologizing for tryna keep her safe. Now I gotta deal with my girl, whose brother may not make it because she wanted to be fucking sneaky. She's six months pregnant and I can't imagine how it's going to affect my child. GOT DAMMIT MARI! WHY DIDN'T YOU JUST LISTEN?" He yelled and stormed out the room.

"He's right."

"What?" Levion asked and came over to me.

"I should've listened to him. If I did, Jose wouldn't be fighting for his life. Daddy, he died in front of me, twice."

"Mari." My mom rubbed my forehead and my brothers all had a sad face.

"You can't control what would've happened. I mean you shouldn't have hit a cop but the other stuff was unavoidable. Honey look…"

"Let me speak to my daughter in private." My father spoke in a firm tone and everyone stepped out the room.

Once the door closed my father took a seat on the side of the bed. I moved over a little to give him more space. He wasn't 100% better and I didn't want him falling off.

He stared at me for a few minutes, which made me a tad bit uncomfortable. I don't know what it is about a girl and her father, but these moments are always precious, even if the situation is fucked up.

I sat up, wrapped my arms around him and cried my eyes out. I cried for Jose, Jocelyn who is probably going through it, and my brothers who each had some sort of turmoil going on in their lives.

"Mari stop crying." He rubbed my back and handed me tissue to wipe my face.

"Daddy if I left Jose alone and she came back, maybe he wouldn't have been shot."

"Nonsense child. Whoever the cop bitch is, is obviously crazy and I believe your story."

"You do?"

"Yes. Something about her rubs me the wrong way and it's not because she's having you arrested for hitting her. She is coo coo upstairs." He pointed to my head.

"Even if it weren't you Jose was with, she'd still do the same. Mari listen." I laid back on the bed.

"You love this Jose guy and each of your brothers minus Rakim all said, he's crazy over you."

"I do love him daddy."

"Then fight for him Mari." I gave him a crazy look.

"Don't let those other women break up what the two of you took time building. It's what they want in hopes he'll give them a chance."

"What about what Rakim said? If I leave him alone then…"

"Then they win and you'll be heartbroken. Is that what you want?" I shook my head no.

"When we pick you up from jail, I'll have Dash bring you up here to see him. It may be hard because of cops being involved, but you can at least try."

"Jail?"

49

"Oh yea, you're going. Our lawyer is waiting so don't think you'll be there long."

"Do I have to go?"

"Absolutely. You're going to give them your story and then, we're going to sue the pants off the police department for having a lunatic on the force."

"But I didn't get shot."

"No but she knew about Jose's relationship with you and followed you to the doctors. *That's harassment.* She yelled out a man had a gun as he stood next to you. *That's putting public safety at risk and calling out false accusations.* And she knew you were pregnant, which makes her liable for almost losing my grandbaby." I felt the monitors on my stomach. This entire time I paid no attention to it and assumed I lost it because no one mentioned it.

"You started bleeding but they said the baby was fine and that stress and most likely fighting did it. However; you were defending your man so I understand, otherwise; I'd be upset about you fighting with my grandbaby inside." He winked and I had him tell the officers we could go. I wanted to get it over with. He walked to the door and everyone came in.

"I'll ride in the car with you." Efrain said. My father demanded one of them go with me and since they were petrified of my brothers, my dad is the only one who was allowed.

"He's gonna be fine Mari." I stared out the back window as the officer pulled away from the hospital.

"I hope so." I rested my head on his shoulder and sent a prayer to God making sure Jose was safe. I don't know what I'd do if he didn't make it.

Jocelyn

"He hasn't woken up yet Mari." It's been two days since my brother was shot and he has yet to open his eyes. The bullet was less than an inch from his heart and the other one almost shattered his sternum. The doctors said he's not in a coma and the reason he's still asleep, is because the amount of medication they had to use are still running through his system. The doctor said, he should wake up soon.

"I'll be right there."

"NO! Mari stay where you are. I can't take the chance of her getting to you. My brother would kill me if she did anything to you."

Mari was arrested for assaulting a police officer and even though they tried to keep her for longer than the few hours she was there, they couldn't. Whoever their lawyer is, ripped the captain a new asshole and is already in the process of suing them.

He contacted me yesterday on behalf of Jose and opened a claim against the department for him as well. I know Jose won't care because he's gonna wake up and go after her.

The reason Mari isn't here is because everyone is afraid Dutchess is preying on her. She may have had Jose shot for not taking her back but we all know, Mari is who she really wants and will stop at nothing to get her. I'm not sure why she even returned to bother him when he's made it abundantly clear the day she showed up that he didn't want her. What is it about women and rejection?

"I can't sit at home not knowing if he needs me."

"I understand Mari."

"I'm going to disguise myself as someone else." I had to laugh at her.

"Mari you know there's security at his door and if you're not on the list, no one will let you in."

"ARGHHHHHHHH!" She shouted through the phone and all the guys shook their head. Oh hell yea, half of Newark was here.

Once they heard about him being shot, all hell broke loose. Police departments were riddled with bullets, cops were dodging drive by's and shit was set on fire. My brother was loved by many and in this day and age, everyone hated the police so it should've been expected for something to happen.

"Give me her address." I turned to see Tito standing there. Tito is one of Jose's closest friends. They may not see each other everyday but they spoke four or five times a week. I think he took it the hardest. I mean, he was crying and everything,

"Tito is coming to get you. Mari I'm going to describe him to you."

"Ok." I started giving her a description of what he looked like and the clothes he wore.

"What kind of car you driving?" I asked and gave her that information as well. I also put her number in so he could call her to come out the house.

"Tell her to cover her entire body up as well as her face." I gave her the directions and watched him and two other guys walk out. I wasn't worried about anyone getting to her with them picking her up.

I hung up and focused on my man who sent me a message saying he'd be up later because they may have figured out who attacked his brother. Their family was being hit with so much, I don't know how they're still standing.

****

"Baby wake up please." I lifted my head off the bed. I dosed off waiting on Mari to get here. I opened my eyes to see her wearing an all-black robe or something close to it. Her face was covered with some mask she took off and her eyes were puffy as hell. You could tell she'd been crying.

"Mari?" He whispered and all of us dropped our mouths. Was Jose waiting to hear her voice?" We've been tryna get him to wake up for two days and nothing. She comes in and BAM! He wakes right up.

"Yes baby, its me." She was about to get in the bed with him but when it moved a little pain etched on his face.

"Where's my sister?"

"She's here and so is Tito, Juan, Raul and a few other people I don't know. How are you feeling?" I pressed the button as he reached out to rub her stomach.

"I almost lost it but our baby is strong like his or her daddy." He let a small grin come across his face.

55

"I love you Mari."

"I love you too baby. I'm so glad you didn't leave me. I missed you so much." She broke down crying harder as he held her hand. Shit, my eyes watered watching their interaction. I don't know what she'd do if he didn't make it or vice versa. These two had the perfect love story and all of us witnessed how deep it was in this room.

"Welcome back Mr. Alvarado." Everyone moved out the way when the doctor stepped in with a nurse.

"You have sixty stitches in your chest and now that you're awake, I want to send you for more test to make sure there's no fragments left inside." He lifted the bed a little and you saw him squeeze Mari's hand.

"You ok babe?" He told her yes but each of us knew he didn't want her worrying. The doctor said he was putting in the paperwork to get his tests done right away. He and the nurse excused themselves.

"Tito, I don't need to say a word." I knew it meant he wanted everyone looking for Dutchess.

"Not at all." He went over to hug my brother gently and so did the others.

"Can I talk to my sister in private?"

"I'm gonna go Jose." Mari kissed his lips.

"NO!"

"Baby I have to. Let Jocelyn fill you in on why." He glanced over at me and I put my head down.

"Have Tito take you."

"He's the one who brought me. I'll call you when I get to the house. I love you." They kissed again and you could tell neither of them wanted to let the other go. I yelled for Tito to come take her out. He had her cover up again and promised to get her home safe.

"Why can't she stay?" He asked and his face got tight when I revealed Dutchess looking for her.

"Where is Dutchess?" He maneuvered his way in the bed, trying to get comfortable.

"They have her in some witness protection shit but we think she still has eyes on Mari. Everyone has been scared to bring her up here, but I wish we did because you opened your eyes the minute she spoke." He smiled.

"I heard some of the guys speaking right before she came in. It just took hearing her voice to physically open them. I was more excited to see her because I didn't know if Dutchess did anything to her." I put my head down.

"What?"

"Mari was arrested and…"

"WHAT?" He shouted and the machines went crazy. He held his chest and began coughing.

"Relax Jose. She was only there for a few hours and her family went with her."

"She should've never been down there."

"Ummmm." I began fidgeting with my hands. *Why did I have to be the one to tell him everything?*

"Um what Jocelyn?"

"She beat Dutchess up and they arrested her for assaulting an officer."

"I'm gonna kick Mari's ass. I told her to stop fighting with my baby in her stomach."

"When she saw them shoot you, I don't think it dawned her not to. Jose, she was scared and clearly not thinking."

"I get it but damn."

"However; she needed her ass beat and oh, Rakim found out the two of you are together. It's a mess."

"Did he touch her?"

"I don't think so. Jose, Rakim is my baby's father." And just like that he went silent. I figured I may as well tell him everything now. No need in hiding.

"He's the one who gave you the disease?" I nodded my head yes.

"I'm not happy with it because he gave you something but if that's who you want then, I'll respect it. However; I don't give a fuck who he is or how much weight his name carries. If he puts his hands on you or does that shit again, we're gonna have a fucking problem." I didn't say anything because he had every right to feel the way he did.

The two of us spoke a little longer and decided he would stay at Mari's place with me. After the news broke, reporters and lawyers have been calling my phone and the neighbors said there were newspaper people at the house. I'm sure everyone wants the exclusive. He asked me to have Tito and Juan come in and help him in the bathroom to clean up.

It was a struggle getting him out the bed because of the pain he was in. Once he got back in, he asked me to call Mari back, spoke to her for a few minutes, pressed the button for medication and he was out like a light. I kissed his cheek and smiled as he slept. I loved my brother dearly and almost gave up on him getting better. I know it's wrong but two bullets to the chest is serious and I thought he'd die.

"You ready?" Rakim asked when I answered the phone. He was downstairs in the lobby and only planned on coming up if I weren't ready. I didn't want him around Jose right now anyway.

Although Tito and him had been speaking a lot about finding Dutchess, he never came in the room. It's funny how Mari never disclosed their relationship to him and here he is tryna help them find her. It's probably more for me and Mari but who cares. Any and all help to find the crazy bitch is appreciated.

Efrain

"Ok Mr. Davis, let's start over." Dr. Miller said and sat across from me as I laid on the chair. My arms were folded and I had my eyes facing the ceiling. I only came because my father said, if I didn't he was gonna make her come to me.

"How are you today?"

"Fine! Next question."

"How's your sister doing?"

"Great! Keep going."

"Ummm ok. Have you had any nightmares lately?"

"No. Is the meeting over?" I turned to look at her with a fake smile and sat up quickly. She removed her glasses and I have to say she's much prettier without them.

"Why you wear those coke bottle looking glasses?" She busted out laughing.

"I'll have you know, I can see very well with these. Plus, there's no prescription in them."

"What?"

"Nope." She shook her head laughing.

"Why you wearing them?"

"Believe it or not, a lotta men who come through these doors hit on me, more than I care to say. So I try to make myself look unattractive as possible to get them to speak to me and not my chest, legs or ass." She stood and walked over to her desk.

She is a big boned woman but not fat. Her legs are thick, she had a small stomach and her breasts are definitely big and juicy just the way I like, but I never paid any attention until she said it. Her clothes were fitted and not tight like most women and you could tell she had her shit together by all the degrees hanging on the wall.

"You have no idea some of the things men say to me." She turned the television on and sat at her desk.

"What are you doing?"

"Oh, I figured you're not ready to talk so I'll eat my lunch, and watch some news until the session is over."

"Really?" She opened the mini refrigerator, grabbed two Tupperware's out and placed one in the microwave. She

62

took the top off the other and there was a nice-looking salad inside. I stood and made my way to where she sat.

"You want some?"

"Not no damn rabbit food, but what's in the microwave?"

"Rabbit food?"

"Yea. Salad is only lettuce and some other shit they eat." She waved me off and went to get the other food out the microwave. There were a few pieces of chicken, macaroni and cheese and corn. My stomach began rumbling so she passed me a fork and had me sit. She grabbed a paper plate and put a small amount on mine.

The two of us sat there in our own thoughts. The news was on and they spoke about the constant violence going on in Newark and Englewood due to Jose Alvarado being shot for no reason by cops. The destruction was crazy and I didn't feel bad, especially; after finding out it was over his ex who couldn't move on.

I know Mari has been going through it too because they didn't want her at the hospital in case the woman showed up.

She did tell me his friends brought her there and he woke up after hearing her voice. Rakim can be mad all he wants but the way I see it is, Jose ain't going nowhere.

"Do you think I can love a woman after the things I been through?" I lifted the fork to my mouth and savored the flavor of the macaroni and cheese. This shit was delicious.

"Mr. Davis, I think you can love who you want. However; you keep trying to escape these demons that have become more and more dangerous to you and may to others."

"What you mean?"

"The last time you were here, you almost beat yourself up." I sucked my teeth because she didn't have to mention it.

"You're waking up in cold sweats and turning to drugs and alcohol to cope. No woman, at least not a real one will deal with a broken man." I looked over at her.

"You think I'm broken?" She wiped her mouth, tossed the napkin on her plate and picked the soda up to drink.

"I do and it's my job to assist you in putting the pieces back together but it's not going to work with you constantly being silent."

"You're right."

"I know." I sucked my teeth again.

"You think I got these degrees for nothing. Man, you better recognize how smart this woman is." She pointed to herself and I started laughing. She stood and kneeled in front of me.

"Mr. Davis you've wasted years holding this pain in and it's time for you to let it out."

"I'm not ready." She held my hands in hers.

"You're never gonna be ready, which is why you have to do just do it." She ran her hand down my face and smiled. A few seconds went by and neither of us said a word.

"Umm. I apologize." She rose to her feet and so did I.

"Apologize for what?" I pulled her closer, parted her lips and we engaged in bad client/ doctor behavior. Her arms were now around my neck and I had her leaning against the desk. She let her hands go under my shirt as I caressed her breasts under hers.

KNOCK! KNOCK!

"Shit." She pushed me off and attempted to fix her clothes.

"Bro, you ready?" Levi stepped in.

"Well, well, well. What do we have here?" Dr. Miller was embarrassed and trying her hardest to put her shirt back in her pants. This nigga had a big ass grin on his face.

"What the fuck you want?"

"Nigga don't get mad at me because your session up and were about to hit the doctor off."

"Shut yo stupid ass up."

"I'm sorry Mr. Davis. It was very unprofessional of us to partake in such an intimate action."

"Why you talking all proper and shit? If you wanna fuck him, go ahead."

"Shut up bro." The doctor covered her mouth.

"Levi come on. I wanna see Mari before. Well, what do we have here?" George came in smiling.

"Nothing. Let's go."

"It don't look like nothing. Missy over there looks flushed and her shirt is hanging out a little. What did I miss babe?"

"I think..." I cut him off before both of them started talking shit.

"Bye Dr. Miller. I'll call for the next appointment." I pushed them out, closed the door and kept walking down the stairs. Both of them kept asking me if we fucked.

"He's about to go jerk off George; watch."

"Oh my God, Levi. Don't say that." They were in the front seat talking like I wasn't there.

"I'm serious. You had to see his face. He was mad as hell I came in. He's definitely going to need a release after all these years of not getting none."

"Yo, can you speed and get my ass home." George was hysterical laughing and Levi wouldn't shut the hell up. Thank goodness it didn't take but ten minutes to drop me off because any longer in the car with them, I probably would've blacked out. I slammed the door and started walking to my door.

"Call her over to finish you off. It's the least she can do for getting you all hot and bothered." George yelled out and Levi pulled off. I yelled out *fuck you* to them and went in my house. What a fucking day!

✱✱✱✱✱✱✱✱✱✱✱✱✱✱✱✱✱✱

"Calm down Efrain." Dr. Miller or should I say Geri told me as we stood in the kitchen of my parents' house.

Ever since the day at the office two weeks ago, she got me to open up more and convinced me today is the day, to inform my family about the trauma. My parents were fully aware but my siblings had no clue.

"What if they laugh or make fun of me?"

"They won't Efrain. They love you." I nodded and glanced at my phone going off. She picked her glass of water up and watched me look at the video sent to me.

"Is that what I think it is?" She snatched the phone out my hand and watched in horror. Someone sent the video of what happened and told me I better not tell anyone what they did or the video would be on the internet.

68

"It's time." She handed the phone back and pushed me in the living room. All my brothers were there. Mari sat under my dad with the phone in her hand and my mom had Kingston on her lap.

Ding! Dong!

"Dash can you get the door?" My mom asked and he gave her a weird look. He got up and did it.

"GENNY!" We all looked at Genesis standing at the door. Her and my brother were in a trance staring at each other. She picked Kingston up and he laid his head on her shoulder.

"Ummm, I didn't know you would be here."

"Why are you here?"

"Your mom called and mentioned you were having a family meeting and she didn't think Kingston should be present." He looked over at my mom who had a smile on her face.

"I tried to get here before you. I'm sorry but she asked if I could take him for a few. If it's a problem, I can take him out in the back until you're done."

"Nah, he misses you."

69

"I missed him too." She kissed his forehead and went to turn around.

"When you're ready to hear the truth Dash, you know how to find me." She leaned in and pecked his lips. All of us were shocked he didn't black out.

Over the last week he was still going off about Nika and Manny saying she wanted to rob him. We all knew it wasn't true because Genesis didn't come off that way. My father didn't even feel that way and he's the one who told Dash to leave Nika alone when he first met her.

"I'll be back." He walked away and went out the back door.

"Give him some time Genesis." My mom gave her a hug.

"I'm trying but I miss him so much." She let a few tears fall.

"He loves you and doesn't know how to handle the things he heard."

"But I would never do those things to him."

70

"We all know honey but you have to see it from his side. You're related to the same woman who betrayed him. It doesn't mean he thinks you're guilty, he just needs to find out why they'd say you are."

"I understand. Can you tell him I love him?" My mom gave her another hug and told her she would.

"Let's go Kingston. I missed you so much." She closed the door and my mom went to get Dash for this meeting, I felt was stupid. Geri rubbed my shoulders and Mari had a big grin on her face.

"What?"

"I didn't say a word. Come sit by me brother unless you don't wanna leave her side."

"Everybody got jokes." I sat next to her and Geri sat across, next to my mother and now Dash who came in. She told me anytime I felt unsure to look at her for confirmation. She said, it's to let me know its ok to finish.

"Ok. Everyone let me first start off by saying thank you for coming. Your brother and son's progress are all we're worried about. Dashier, Demaris, Levion and Rakim, I want

71

you to know that what he's going to say is going to throw you for a loop and I need for each of you to stay seated and quiet. I'm asking that you allow him to finish because as we all know, the minute he stops and shuts down, he may not speak on it again. If we want him to moved forward in his life we have to give him our full attention with no interruptions."

"It's that bad?" Dash asked and stared at me. I put my head down and felt Mari rubbing my back.

"Efrain the floor is all yours." I took a deep breath and looked at my parents, who both nodded and then Geri who gave me a reassuring smile. In the last week, she got me to tell her the full story of what happened. I had been giving her bits and pieces but the specific day, she ran in the bathroom because I was so angry, she got scared I'd hit her.

"Ok, so a long time ago when I went to one of Gavin's parties some shit happened." I started from the beginning and all of them sat there listening to this horrid story I had to tell.

"The fuck you mean like the others?" One dude laughed when I asked.

"Make sure the door is locked." Bobby said and outta nowhere I felt mad hands on me.

"Get the fuck off me." I started swinging or thought I was until the Bobby guy hit me hard as fuck. I don't even know how I got on the floor or why my ass was naked. I do know what happened next brought my ass to tears.

"Ahh shit man, Your ass tight as fuck." He rammed himself inside me. I tried my hardest to get this nigga off but whoever the other ones were, held me down tight.

One by one, at least four niggas took turns raping me. No matter how much I yelled, cursed and even tried to fight, nothing stopped them. You could hear them laughing each time one came inside me. One pulled out and nut all over my back. The shit went on for what felt like hours until someone knocked on the door. By that time, I was half dead or wished I was.

"Have any of you seen Efrain?" I heard Nicole's voice.

"He's busy right now."

"Busy? Please don't tell me you did that to him." I could hear panic in her voice. Did she know they did this to everyone?

"It's your fault Nicole. You never should've left me."

Left him? I didn't even know she used to fuck with him.

"Move Bobby." I heard him laughing and felt her rubbing my face.

"Are you ok Efrain? Let me get you outta here."

"Nah, we not done. Beat it."

"NOOOOO! Let him go." She shouted and I heard a loud thump.

"Take your stupid ass downstairs and if you open your mouth to anyone, I'll kill you and your family." You heard the door slam and that was it. I blacked out when someone flipped me over and began giving me head. I woke up naked in my car the next day, drove home and locked myself in the room.

Over the next two weeks, I was so traumatized, I drank, took drugs and fucked up the rest of my life. I didn't wanna leave the house because I became afraid they'd catch me again and I wouldn't be able to fight them off.

I contemplated suicide various times which is why mommy called me everyday, all day. And pops stopped speaking to me for a while because I never told. The only

74

reason I'm mentioning it now is beside me needing to move on, I need help finding them." I looked and all of my brothers and even Mari had tears coming down their face.

"I should've told y'all a long time ago but I was ashamed, embarrassed and most of disgusted with myself for not being able to control the situation. I'm no punk but I couldn't fight them off." I put my head down.

"Efrain what they did was wrong. You can't blame yourself." Mari hugged me tight and wouldn't let go.

"That was good Efrain. Let's give your family a moment to let everything sink in before we go on." It wasn't anything else to really tell but she wanted me to ask if they had questions or some shit.

Dash sat back with his head facing the ceiling. Levion had a snarl on his face and Rakim looked like he was ready to kill the world. Mari held my hand and wiped the tears falling down my own face. I wasn't crying for what happened to me because those days are over. I shed tears because my family finally knew the reason for my actions. They knew it wasn't attention seeking or me doing it just because. I pulled my cell out my pocket, went to my messages and hit play.

"GET OFF ME!" You could hear me shouting on the phone as the video played.

"Tha fuck is that?" Rakim came over and snatched the phone out my hand. His eyes grew wide and he let the phone hit the ground. Mari picked it up and became hysterical and I don't even know how Dash and Levi took it because my mom was hugging me tight.

"I'm so proud of you son. I know how hard it was." Now I was hugging her tighter. It definitely felt good getting that shit off my chest.

"Yo, Levi." Rakim shouted.

"I'm already on it." He picked his phone up and started making calls. I heard him say something about tracing the phone number to whoever sent the video.

"Who attacked you at the store?" Dash stood in front of me.

"Gavin and Bobby is the one who tried to cut my throat. I don't even know how they found me that night."

76

"GAVIN!" Rakim shouted.

"Yea. He had me selling dope for him on the side to make more money. I refused a few times but once he showed me the video, I had no choice. I couldn't embarrass my family like that and let him leak the video. The day they attacked me at the store he said something about being a boss, and that he had to beat my ass, the way his boss did. I didn't know you were his boss at the time, otherwise; I would've told you." When Mari mentioned him being the biggest dealer around, I put two and two together.

"You should've told us Efrain but don't you worry. We're about to make sure none of them bother you again and you can cancel Nicole too." I nodded. She may not have known they were going to get me but the fact she knew they've done it to others is just as bad.

"Raphael has connections in the police department. What's their last names?" I gave as much info as I could to them and watched all of them get on their phones.

"Efrain if Jose were better he'd be helping too." Mari hugged me again.

77

"I know sis. I also know how much you're missing him. Have they let you go see him?"

"I snuck up there once but I haven't been back. Do you know reporters, lawyers and a bunch of other people have been at their house? It's so bad, Jocelyn has been staying with me but the good thing is, no one can get to him at the hospital."

"Thanks sis for always being there."

"There's never a time I won't. I am My Brother's Keeper."

"We all are." Dash came in and gave me a hug, and so did Rakim and Levi. I know people may think I should've said something sooner but it's not as easy to tell those things as one may think.

"Thank you Dr. Miller but he still needs therapy." I heard my pops telling her.

"Yes and after you and him sleep together for the first time, make sure you help him deal with that."

"Ma, really?" I pulled her away.

"Son, we all noticed how you two are so no need to fight it. Honey, please be fragile with him in the bedroom. I'm not sure he's been with a woman since."

"Yo, I'm out." Geri covered her mouth laughing as I escorted her to the door.

"Don't you worry Efrain. I'm gonna be extra careful with you and to make it better, I'm gonna do something special when it happens." My dick jumped and I had to grab myself.

"I'ma see you later." She kissed me and I walked her out. Watching her pull off made me realize I wasted enough time on the past and needed to focus on the future, with or without her.

"Don't get her pregnant the first night. I know it's been a while and you probably wanna feel some raw pussy."

"Bye Rakim."

"I'm just fucking with you but I'm proud of you bro. I know it was hard and my love don't change for you." He hugged me and said he had to go grab Jocelyn some food.

"I wish you would've told us, but I understand. I love you bro." Dash gave me a hug and left too. Levi and Mari both did the same. I closed the door and went to find my parents.

They were being fresh like always. I shook my head and went

upstairs to lay down. I'm glad the hard part is over.

Jose

"I'm over this shit man." I took the hospital covers off my legs and tried to get up.

It's been almost a month since being shot and I haven't seen my girl except the day I opened my eyes. Well I've seen her on face time and we speak every night and day but it's not the same. I missed the shit outta her and I know she felt the same because she cried about wanting to lay next to me.

We were so used to being around each other it was taken a toll on us not to be. Even when I put her ass in time out, we still saw one another at work. This shit is straight torture.

"What you need?" Tito asked and they all looked at me.

"Tell the nurse I'm leaving TODAY!"

"It's about time bro. I was getting tired of sitting up here and your cousin is driving me crazy for staying up here." I laughed because him and my cousin have been together for years.

She's just like me when it came to wanting to be under him, the same way I wanted to be under my girl. But being my

81

best friend first, he stayed by my side and I appreciated the fuck outta him for it.

Jocelyn and Mari did too because they knew he wouldn't allow anyone to get me. Juan is the same and sat with me during the day if Tito had something to do. They've been putting in work tryna find Dutchess. The cops had her hidden well but forgot to hide her family.

Juan and Raul took her parents out the same day my sister mentioned me being shot and who was responsible. Tito found her brother a few days ago and sad to say, he's taking a dirt nap as well. She had a sister we haven't been able to locate but I'm gonna have Mari's brother find him. He definitely can work magic on the computer.

He broke into the store security where Efrain was attacked and saw what took place. The only reason they had no idea who the people were, is because how dark it was. The facial recognition couldn't pick it up. I guess it don't matter now since Mari mentioned Efrain finally broke down and told everything. I didn't even ask what it was but I could tell it was traumatizing. If she wants to fill me in, I'll let her otherwise I

82

won't bother her about it. Sometimes family stuff, stays within the family.

"Mr. Alvarado the doctor is coming in." The nurse spoke over the intercom as I continued putting my clothes on slow. I ended up with an infection somehow, which is why I stayed so long.

"How are you today?" The doctor stepped in as I slipped my foot in the sneakers Mari sent up. She wanted me dressed everyday in case someone came to see me.

"Good. I need to get outta here."

"I was going to discharge you tomorrow but today is fine. The infection is gone and your tests are normal. I also know your anxious to get home to your woman. Do you know she calls me everyday I'm working to find out when you're going home?" I busted out laughing and the guys shook their head.

"I wanna surprise her so if she calls today don't mention it." He agreed, did a few vital checks and cleared me to go. I still had to take some medication and he gave me a prescription for pain. I probably won't use them but they're good to have.

The nurse brought a wheelchair in for me to go downstairs. She tried to get Tito to go ahead and get the car but he refused and took the elevator with us. Juan and Raul left a few minutes before us.

"Do you want to get the car now?" She asked Tito and he looked at me.

"No. I can walk from here."

"Mr. Alvarado I'm supposed to put you in a car." She flirted and smiled.

"I'm gonna leave with him because if my girl shows up and catches you flirting the way you are, I won't be able to stop her from beating your ass."

"Oh you got one of those women." She sucked her teeth.

"Yup and she has one of those niggas so don't even think of saying anything slick because I'll run straight up in your mouth and still go home to her." She swung the wheelchair hard as hell and rolled her eyes. Tito was cracking up.

"Fuck her." He took his time walking with me and made sure I didn't fall. The medication in my system definitely had me feeling light headed.

"You good?" I put my head on the seat.

"Yea. Just get me home."

"A'ight. Let me grab your medicine first."

"Yo, can you pick some flowers up for her?"

"Bro, really?"

"Hell yea really. I'm tryna keep my girl and I want her to remember why she loves me."

"Corny ass nigga. I swear if your cousin start asking me to do the same, I'm kicking your ass." He and I drove to the store laughing and joking. I stayed in the car when he went inside tho.

Mari called me twice and each time I sent her to voicemail. I know she's gonna start worrying but I wanted to surprise her and I can't if she keeps calling. Her ass will guess

I left with her nosy ass. I did send her a text telling her the doctor was in the room.

"I'll see you later." Tito kept the car running and we gave each other the man hug thing.

"Call me tomorrow." I told him and opened the door.

"Yea right. Mari is about to fuck the shit outta yo ass. I'll call you in a few days."

"Whatever." I laughed because he's most likely right. I can't even tell you how many nights we had phone sex. Well she did more than I. My arms worked fine but I could only please myself a few times due to the pain.

I stepped in the house knowing she was at work and moved around slow. Dash allowed her to come as long as she had security there. Ever since Nika and Genesis ex showed up, he hired two more security dudes just in case. Both of them stayed upstairs where our offices were. It made me feel at ease and him too. If anyone got passed the two downstairs they wouldn't get far upstairs.

I took all my clothes off and hopped in the shower. I was able to bathe in the hospital but nothing made you feel better than your own. My chest still had pain here and there but overall, movement wasn't as bad. I didn't have to worry about my stiches busting because he took them out yesterday.

When I finished getting myself together, I went downstairs to find something to eat. Mari cooked for me everyday and had Juan or Tito pick it up and bring it.

I pulled out the fried fish, corn and mashed potatoes from yesterday and heated it up. I sat there alone thinking of ways to kill Dutchess. I also thought about the conversation Rakim and I are gonna have. He gave my sister a disease and got her pregnant, which means we'll have the same blood running through my niece or nephew. Then, there's Mari who's my woman and he can be mad all he wants but ain't nobody breaking up for him.

I cleaned my mess up, went upstairs and laid down. The bed was comfortable as hell and I fell straight to sleep.

****

"Mmph shit Mari." She woke me up giving me head and a nigga appreciated it so much, I came instantly.

"I missed you so much baby." She climbed on top slowly and I could feel how wet she was down below. Her hair was dripping down and I could smell the pear body wash she used in the shower.

"I missed you too ma. Sit up here." I used my arms to move her up to my face and she yelled at me but quieted down the minute my mouth touched her nub. I placed the tip of my tongue in the middle of her pussy. Her clit began to swell up and all her nectar slid down my face. After the third one she began shaking.

"Fuck Jose." She rolled on her side and had her back to me. I felt my man growing at the sight of her juicy ass. I stood and pulled her to the edge.

"Take it easy."

"I am but I need you Mari. It's been a month and my dick is yearning to be inside you." She lifted on her elbows and slid down so I could enter with ease.

"Got damn, I love the fuck outta you." I stroked her slow and steady as she grinded under me.

"Jose please don't ever cheat on me." I stopped and stared at her crying. I took her hands in mine and pulled her up.

"We'll discuss the irrelevant shit later but know I would never cheat on you. There's no need and I think you know it."

"I did until she said…" I cut her off by crashing my lips on her and continuing to beat the pussy up.

"Yes baby, yes. Don't stop." I had both of her legs in the air, spread wide open as I dug and dug until it felt like I hit wall. Whatever it was had Mari's body spazzing and her juices were squirting out like crazy.

"Yea ma. Give me all that good shit. Mmmm fuck yea." I went deeper again and this time she clenched her muscles together and made me cum so hard, I fell on the bed.

"I won't let another woman have you Jose." I turned to stare at her. She smiled and let her four fingers run down the side of my face.

"I will kill any bitch for tryna get what I get."

"Mari you're not a killer." She smiled.

"For you and my family, I'll do whatever is necessary."

"Damn! I don't know what to say." I had no idea she felt that strong. I know she was in love but wow. She's talking about killing for me.

"Would you still kill for me?"

"In a heartbeat."

"Then its only right I do the same for you." She stood up and bent down in front of me with her ass cheeks spread open. I could see her juices leaking out and my dick sprung right back to life.

"No woman has ever had me strung off her pussy but you. Shitttttt." I could sit my dick inside her all day and be fine, that's how good she felt.

"Joseeeeeee. I'm cumming again. Yesssssss." She screamed out as I gathered up more strength and fucked the shit outta her. This time we went at it longer and I must say, it's always worth it.

"I'm two and half months." She let my hand rest on her stomach after we finished. I never got the chance to ask when she came to see me.

"I'm happy you're gonna be my child's mother." I kissed the top of her shoulder.

"And I'm happy you'll be the father."

"I know its old fashioned but I wanna be married before the baby comes." I turned her over to see if she were serious and she was.

"I'll meet you at the justice of the peace in two days." I kissed her lips.

"Why two days?"

"I need to get you a ring and do it the right way."

"I don't need a ring."

"The hell if you don't. Nigga's should know you're off the market."

"I been off the market let you tell it."

"You sure have but I still want a ring on you." She nodded and got closer to me. The two of us stayed in the same position all night. I'm gonna give her what she wants and make her my wife and right after; I'll be on the fucking prowl to find this bitch because she will die by my fucking hands.

Demaris

"Let's talk Mari." Jose grabbed my hand and led me in the living room. I came home last night expecting to FaceTime him for sex and he was asleep in the bed. I couldn't help myself and made sure to please him the way he liked.

"About?"

"Dutchess." I sucked my teeth.

"Don't suck your teeth when tears streamed down your face in the middle of sex. Obviously, it bothers you so let's get it out the way." I plopped down on the couch and folded my arms like the spoiled brat I am.

"What do you wanna know?" He laid on the couch opposite of me and I could tell he felt some pain. I went in the kitchen to grab him a bottle of water and one of the Vicodin's the doctor prescribed. I handed it to him and he kept it in his hand. He wanted to have this conversation before the meds kicked in.

I stared down at this beautiful Hispanic man and smiled. He was the perfect man for me and I almost lost him over a bitch who don't know how to let go. I definitely understand

92

sexually why she wanted him because like I told him last night, I refused to allow another woman to have him. The thought of him even kissing another makes my stomach crawl.

I sat down next to him but on the floor. He wanted me to lay but I declined. His chest rose up and down slowly and I tried to keep my eyes off the print in his basketball shorts but it was no use. The crazy part is, I have no problem with him being the only man to ever bed me. Jose more than satisfies me and I guarantee no one will ever top him.

"Babe we don't have to talk about it. You're in pain and..."

"Yes we do because if not you'll always be wondering. What do you want to know?"

"Whatever you wanna tell me." He turned over.

"Dutchess and I were a couple straight outta high school. She was cool as hell, and the two of us got along for the most part. Unfortunately, she started discussing more and more about how she wanted to be a cop and one day a detective. Me; being a nigga off the street didn't think we should be together because I never wanted her to investigate me."

"Investigate you?"

"Eventually, she would become a detective and I didn't know if I was making a career outta being a street hustler. I also didn't wanna jeopardize anything she worked hard for." I nodded.

"Anyway, she started becoming crazy and blowing up on people everywhere we went. Tito's sister, Juan's family members and even Raul's aunt who is young like us, felt the wrath of Dutchess. They didn't fight but there were a lotta times it could've happened." I turned my face up because she was doing too much.

"It became too much for me and I don't do drama unless I have to." He moved his legs off the couch and sat up.

"Mari, we couldn't even have a good time when we went out because it's was always something."

"Did you sleep with her?" He looked at me.

"Of course I slept with her. What kind of question is that?"

"I didn't mean it like that. I guess I'm asking did you make love to her?"

"Yes, because at the time I was in love with her. I think it's why she is the way she is towards me."

"What you mean?"

"Just like you don't want another woman touching me, she felt and obviously still feels the same. No woman wants to allow another to feel what they did. The crazy thing about it is, you are two different women and I make love to you way different."

"What you mean?"

"You were a virgin, which means I taught you everything and you had no problems bringing out your inner freak."

"Nasty." I smiled thinking about all the stuff we do.

"Don't get me wrong. She did a lot in the bedroom too but nowhere near as much as you and I."

"I don't understand."

"When I make love to you we have a connection and because of it we go hard for each other. Nothing is off limits with us and because it's not, it makes sex a hundred times better."

"I guess."

"Look Mari." He sat up and had me get off the floor and sit on his lap.

"Dutchess is my past and will never, ever be in my future. For one… she'll be dead soon and two… I'm about to marry you. Therefore; no other woman will get what you get."

"Did you cheat on her?" He blew his breath in the air.

"No, but I can see why she thought I did." I looked at him.

"I broke up with her and she said, we'd never be over. Instead of leaving her alone completely, my dumb ass continued sleeping with her. I never told her we were back together or anything like that but I didn't want her to sleep with anyone else. She found out about this chick I slept with and got mad. She accused me of cheating on her and when I mentioned we weren't a couple, she didn't wanna hear it. All she kept saying was, you should've never slept with me again and some other shit."

"But you didn't say y'all were back together."

"Exactly! However, she saw things differently. After she beat the girl up, *real bad too.* I never touched her again. It didn't matter how much she cried, begged, and pleaded. She had me at my wits end and I was done. I ended up having to stay on the block extra time just to keep the chick from going to the police on Dutchess. It would've ruined her chances at being a cop."

"What does you being on the block have to do with her? I'm lost."

"I had to pay the chick she beat up 10k to remain quiet."

"Oh my. Well, you don't have to pay that for me."

"Hell no. Me and you are forever." I leaned in to kiss him and felt his phone going off. I glanced down at the same time he did and it was a message from Talia. He opened it and the bitch sent a nasty video of herself and I was pissed.

"Did you make love to her too? Is that why she's the way she is?" I watched as he blocked and deleted her number.

It should've been done but I didn't even waste my time arguing over it because I know he hasn't been with or around her.

"Nah. I only fucked her but you know she loves the way my dick curves and how I make her cum." I tried to get up quick and he sat me down.

"I'm just playing. I don't know what the fuck wrong with her but I'm gonna make sure she doesn't bother you again either."

"You better."

"Mari, I never expected anyone from my past to harass you and I apologize for it. I know its bringing a lotta emotions out for you and it's not my intention to see you hurt or fighting. All I wanna do is make you cum hard and smile."

"Jose."

"I'm serious. You came in my life at the right time and to be honest, I thought you'd be a good fuck and I'd move on. But after getting to know you, I wanted more." I smiled.

"You're perfect for me and that's some real shit." I turned to straddle him.

"I'm perfect for you Jose?"

"Absolutely." He squeezed my ass over the small shorts I had on and placed his face in the crook of my neck. Both of us were beginning to get aroused.

"Baby your sister may walk in." He slid the seat of my shorts to the side, lifted me up as he pulled his dick out and guided me down slow.

"I promise you have the best, I've ever had Mari. Shitttt." He let his head fall back as I used both of my hands to grab the back of the couch. I watched him bite down on his lip and close his eyes. Each time I went down, I felt him deeper.

"Play with that pussy and cum for me." He stared down as I circled my clit. The pleasure building had me going insane. I loved getting this type of feeling through penetration. It was different and would have me shaking and spazzing out.

"You almost there ma. Keep going." His hand went behind my neck as we kissed feverishly.

"Oh fuck Jose. Yes baby." His dick was twitching inside.

"Let it go Mari." I nodded my head and the two of us got lost in each other. I rested my head on his shoulder and both of us were breathing fast.

"I don't ever wanna think about any man giving you this kinda pleasure."

"Never."

"You're mine forever baby." We began kissing again, when we heard the door opening.

"MARI!" I heard my mother yelling out.

"Oh shit!" Jose grabbed the blanket he brought down from upstairs and covered up. I stood and felt his juices running down my leg. I hauled ass to the bathroom to clean up. I had no idea she was stopping by. That's what we get for fucking anywhere.

****

"So you two are gonna pretend like you weren't having sex in the living room?" My father asked staring at Jose who recently walked in. I ran upstairs, cleaned up and threw some sweats on. He jumped in the shower to play it off but my parents knew better. Actually, I expected my mom to say it but she was too busy pulling food out the bags to cook. Not only did they pop up but now she's about to feed us.

"I apologize sir. We should've been more careful or waited until we got upstairs." I loved how he spoke respectfully to my dad.

"You just admitted to having sex with my daughter?"

"No disrespect Mr. Davis, but she's about to have my child so I know you're well aware we have sex."

"Stop messing with him Dashier." My mom popped him on the shoulder and had Jose and I take a seat at the table with them.

"First let me introduce you. Mommy and Daddy, this is Jose and Jose these are my parents."

"What took you so long bringing him around or did he not want to?"

"Sir, your daughter was struggling with Rakim finding out about our relationship. In doing so she kept putting it off. I told her many times to tell him, especially; since we're going to get married. Oh that reminds me. Do you mind if I marry her?" He took a ring out his pocket and got on his knees.

"Oh my God Jose. When did you get this?" Granted we were supposed to get married tomorrow but I assumed today, we'd get the ring. Instead we laid around most of the day and never made it to the store.

"I had it for a while now and was waiting for the right time to ask." I can't believe he's been waiting to ask me.

"Mari. You are the only woman I want. You're the one I wanna wake up to every morning and the only one, I go to bed to. Like I told you before, you're everything to me and no one will ever take your place. Will you marry me?" I turned to look at my parents. My mom had her hand on her chest with a few tears falling down her face and my dad had a smile on his.

"YES! YES, BABY YES!" I screamed out and watched as he placed this humongous diamond on my finger. I tried to jump in his arms but he stopped me.

"Mari, relax. You know the man is still recovering." My father barked and came over to hug me. He was doing so much better and I was even more ecstatic that he'd be the one walking me down the aisle.

"Congratulations son in law." My dad shook his hand and embraced him. My mom did the same and kissed his cheek.

"Even though this is ass backwards, what are your intentions with my daughter?" My father asked and the two of them began conversing away from me and my mom.

"You look happy Mari."

"I am mommy. I love him so much." I started feeling emotional again.

"And we know he feels the same because your three brothers get a kick outta hearing how crazy is he about you. Did he really snatch you away from another guy at the bank trying to take you out?" I shook my head listening to her tell me the jokes my brothers had on me.

"I'm gonna be a grandmother a few times within the next year. How am I going to have all of them at once?" I laughed at her discussing whose child she'd have and on what days.

"Oh. George and Levi have started the adoption process."

"REALLY?"

"Yea, they came and asked if I thought it was ok. Mari, you know I don't care. Whatever child they adopt, no matter what color will still be my grandbaby. Shit, they already married so why not?"

"Married? What are you talking about?"

"Your mother never could hold a secret." My dad came in with Jose grinning.

"Yea, it happened in the hospital right after he got attacked. And before you get upset; don't."

"But I wanted to be there."

"Honey, George loves you for being his best friend now and Levi does too but this is something they wanted to do. It was in the middle of the night and they didn't want to make anyone get outta the bed. It was only the two of them, us and the preacher."

"Don't you cry." Jose stood behind me.

"Why didn't they want me to come?" I wiped the few

tears.

"Mari stop acting like a brat."

"They're not coming to my wedding then."

"Stop it Mari. You're being ridiculous and if they can't

come then you'll be standing there alone." I snapped my head

to look at Jose.

"Don't look at me like that. Levi will be my brother in

law and George is cool with me too. I want them there so it is,

what it is."

"If my parents weren't here I'd…"

"You'd what?" I felt him tickling my side.

"Stop with those stupid threats."

"Ok. Ok." He almost had me in tears from laughing so

hard.

"Jose, where are you?" We heard Jocelyn yell and

everyone stopped speaking when he walked in.

Rakim

"What's the joke?" I walked in my sister's house expecting to smell food and forgot this nigga was staying with her. I didn't care for them to be together and when he came home from the hospital, Jocelyn told me he'd be staying with her because of the reporters and shit.

"Oh my God Jose you asked. Mari it's beautiful." I glanced over at my sisters' hand and noticed this huge ring on her finger. My parents seemed to be happy, where I wasn't.

"Tha fuck you thinking Mari? Didn't I tell you he wasn't no good?"

"Yo! Who the fuck you talking to? She ain't no bitch off the street nigga." Jose stood and both Jocelyn and Mari got in between.

"She's my sister and you ain't no good for her."

"Says who? You?"

"Damn right me. Got her fighting in the streets and bitches tryna find her. She don't need that kinda bullshit in her life."

"Oh so you passing off diseases and cheating is ok?"

106

"Jose!" Jocelyn shouted and I could tell she was embarrassed.

"Nah fuck that sis. He thinks he can speak to my fiancé anyway he wants. You know I don't play that shit. I know he better not be talking to you that way."

"And if I were?" I moved Jocelyn out the way and he attempted to move Mari but she didn't budge. His strength was limited and whether he can fight or not, I had him at a disadvantage.

"Lucky for you, I can tell you're weak and I'm not the type of nigga to play off it."

"Don't let this fool you." He pointed to his chest.

"Alright you two." My mom pulled me away.

"Rakim ever since you yanked her up in the hospital, you've been very hostile towards her."

"HOLD THE FUCK UP! YOU PUT YOUR HANDS ON HER?" I folded my arms and stared at him.

"Jose please. It's fine." My sister was standing in front of him crying.

"Mari, that shit ain't fine and you know it. I'd never raise my hand to you so don't think because he's your brother it's ok. I may not like who my sister chose but I'd never put my hands on her either. Tha fuck type of shit you on?"

"You ain't no weak nigga, right? If you wanna get it popping then let's go." I wasn't about to let this punk talk shit. He removed his shirt and this time moved Mari out the way.

"THAT'S ENOUGH!" My father barked.

"I think it's time for me to go."

"Jose don't go."

"You begging Mari?"

"Rakim SHUT UP!" Jocelyn yelled and it wasn't until I saw her upset that I listened.

"I'm not ok with this shit Mari. I'm out." He moved passed me but my pops blocked to make sure neither of us swung. I saw him going up the stairs.

WHAP! Mari walked up and smacked the fuck outta me.

"I love you because you're my brother Rakim but right now I can't stand you."

"Mari, he's..."

108

"He's what? No good for me. Just like you're no good for Jocelyn." She shook her head in disgust at me.

"You know he tried to stay away but I pursued him. You're trying to keep a street dude away from me and he isn't even in the streets anymore."

"He used to be and now look. You've been fighting bitches and one is looking for you. Mari you're better than that."

"And Jocelyn can do better than you." She scoffed up a laugh.

"You brought her back a disease, cheated on her, and had her fighting too but you don't see me stepping to her. I'm not questioning anything you do, you know why?"

"Why?"

"Because y'all love each other no matter what and I would never get in the middle of it unless necessary." I noticed how upset she was getting again.

"He proposed to me Rakim and our parents gave him their blessing and what did you do. You ruined a perfectly good day because you like being a fucking asshole."

"Mari." I grabbed the back of her elbow and she snatched away.

"It was nice meeting you and I apologize for disrespecting you. Until next time." Jose spoke to my parents and walked away with Jocelyn behind.

"Where are you going?" She stopped at the door and I saw her pass the keys to Jose.

"I know you have ignorant ways about you but you went overboard for no reason at all."

"You told him I gave you something?" I whispered, still embarrassed he shouted it out in front of my parents.

"He's my brother and all I got Rakim. Of course, I told him. I didn't expect him to mention it and he wouldn't have if you didn't open your mouth and disrespect his woman."

"She's my sister."

"And she's his fiancé. What did you think he'd say after hearing you put hands on her? I know you can't possibly think he'd let it slide."

"That's their business. Why are you leaving?" I tried moving past the conversation because I didn't want her to leave.

"You're right that is their business and you had no right to interfere. And just like your family got you for whatever. I got him. You should know that after seeing me hop in a fight when dudes were jumping him. I am My Brother's Keeper too. Goodbye." Say what you want but I'm always gonna feel as if Mari deserves better. Why wouldn't I?

I didn't even try to go after her. I went to my car and drove to my next destination because truthfully, I had shit to do.

****

BOOM! I let Ced shoot the lock on the door. We usually just kick shit in but his crazy ass wanted to try this new gun he ordered.

"Look what we have here." I yelled out and grabbed the bitch off the couch. She screamed and tried to pry my hands off her.

It didn't take long to find her because she stayed in the area, where everyone else moved, from what the data record showed when Levi and Raphael looked them up. But don't worry. We shall find them too. My brother stepped in and her eyes got big.

"Efrain?"

"Yea it's me. You didn't think I forgot about you." He smirked and walked over to her.

"What are you doing here and why does he have a gun on me?"

"No one here." Ced came out of each room with another one of the workers, Ron.

"I just wanna know why?"

"Why what? Can you ask him to take the gun off me?"

"Nah and you know why, but since you wanna hear it. Why did you let those niggas do that to me?" I heard a bit of sadness in his voice. I told him we'd handle it but he wanted to look each person in their eye before they took their last breath.

"Efrain, I didn't know they had you up there."

"BUT YOU KNEW THE NASTY SHIT THEY DID TO PEOPLE AND NEVER SAID A WORD." Outta nowhere he punched her in the face and her lip split wide open.

"Then, when they told you to leave you could've called the cops but what did you do? Took your ass home and I didn't see or speak to you again until the day of graduation. It's like you avoided me. What kind of girlfriend doesn't check on her man after witnessing the trauma he went through. That's what I wanna know."

"I'm sorry Efrain. I was scared and they threatened to kill my family if I told and..."

"And you knew who my family was. I would've made sure nothing happened to you. But instead, you avoid me like the plague." He kneeled down in front of her.

"I loved you Nicole and you fucked me over."

"I loved you too and if I could change things I would've." He gave her this cynical laugh and stood.

"I don't want her dead yet Rakim."

"Come on Efrain. Let me use my new toy." Ced had the gun on the opposite side of where mine was.

113

"Not yet Ced. I want her locked up so when we get the others. She can witness what they did to me, happen to them and it'll be the last thing she sees before going to hell."

"Efrain please. I'll do anything." She was begging and pleaded. I thought he'd feel bad but he didn't.

"I don't want her to starve. Give her just enough to eat and drink so she'll be alive. Oh and Nicole." She looked up.

"I knew the baby you got rid of wasn't mine because the dates didn't match up."

"I did love you Efrain and it was a mistake."

"They always are. I'll see you soon." He gave her an evil glare and stepped out the apartment.

"Who carrying her big ass out?" Ced asked and looked at me.

"Don't look over here. The only big chick I'm lifting is my baby mama and she won't be that big once my baby comes out." We looked at Ron.

"Hell no, not me. I'm smaller than both of y'all. Get yo ass up and walk." He kicked her in the back and we all busted out laughing.

"Please don't hurt me."

"Get up." She didn't move.

"Fuck this. Ced grab her other foot and Ron make sure her head don't hit the ground on the way."

"Bro her shit big. I don't think I can carry it." I thought Ced was gonna use the bathroom on himself from laughing so hard.

"I'll walk." She stood and once she did, her ass tried to run.

"PHEW!

"Ahhhhhhh." She screamed out. I went over and held the gun under her chin.

"Listen here you dumb bitch. You're gonna walk outta here and if you even think about running I'ma have Ced kill you."

"But he shot me in the leg."

"Bitch, it don't hurt." Ced and Ron were hysterical.

"A'ight y'all on some real shit. Let's get her to the place. Ced make the call for our people to get here and clean up. Ron call up Morris and have him get the spot ready at the warehouse." They did like I asked and this bitch limped, cried and threw up on the way to the van.

I had Ced call up this chick he knew who works at the hospital to take this damn bullet out. Efrain would kill me if she died before seeing the others.

After doing what needed to be done, I called Jocelyn to see if she was coming over and her phone went straight to voicemail. I didn't bother calling and drove home. I could stop by her place but then me and Jose would get into it and I don't feel like hearing her mouth or Mari's.

When I got home, I showered and got in the bed. I felt my phone vibrate and looked to see a message from Jocelyn.

My girl: *I don't care how long I'm mad at you, you better not even think about bringing another bitch over there or going to her house.* I started cracking up.

Me: *Never baby mama. I'll wait as long as you want.*

My girl: *You fucking better. Goodnight.*

Me: *Goodnight and I love you*

My girl: *I love you too*

I put my phone down and rolled over to go to sleep. It still feels weird as fuck being in one relationship and saying I love you. I see now what niggas mean when they say one woman will make you leave everyone else alone. That woman is definitely Jocelyn. She got me to do what no one else has and that's settle down.

Jocelyn

Rakim pissed me off so bad, I couldn't even be around him anymore. Now I'm all for defending your siblings but he was taking it too far. Then to know he put his hands on Mari because of my brother made me angrier. Why is he so hell bent on them not being together? Mari is a good girl like me and can take care of herself; like me. Yet, both of us found love in a man who either is or was in the streets.

Hell no, I've never been with a man like Rakim and if we break up, I probably wouldn't then. It's too much of a hassle tryna figure out if he's cheating or even gonna make it home at night. I know he's not out killing everyday but I'm not naive to the fact that he's done it or will in the future. It's who he is and the man I fell in love with.

What I won't do is sit around and allow him to chastise his sister and continuously come for Jose. I don't care how in love I am. If he comes for my brother, then he's coming for me.

I sent him a text last night that he better not cheat and I meant it. We all know that dirty pussy ho Ranisha is lurking around somewhere. I wouldn't put it past her to try and fuck if

118

she saw him. Of course, I'm beating her ass and killing him in his sleep if he did cheat but that's beside the point. I laid down and went to sleep with so much on my mind. Hopefully, tomorrow will be a better day.

I woke up this morning wanting to talk to Jose about everything that took place over Mari's. When we came in, he went to his room and closed the door. I figured he needed space and probably wanted to take some pain medication. He wasn't addicted but he did use them when needed.

I hopped in the shower, brushed my teeth and got myself ready for the day. I was seven months now and getting bigger by the day. I threw on some pajama pants, a tank top with my bunny slippers and headed downstairs to make us something to eat. Imagine my surprise to see Mari sitting on the island in just one of my brothers' T-shirts. She was feeding him off her plate, like always.

"Well good morning to y'all too." Both of them turned to look at me.

"Damn Jocelyn. Does your stomach grow everyday?"

"Jose don't say that." She popped him on the arm.

"Anyway, when did you get here Mari?" She looked at Jose.

"Don't look at me. I woke up and she was about to place that juicy pussy on my face." Mari's entire face turned red.

"I'm just kidding but I did suck the shit out of it didn't I?"

"I'm gonna stop talking to you in the morning because it's definitely too early for this." I moved past him and checked the microwave for my plate and there it was. Eggs, bacon, pancakes and grits.

"I did come in when it was late but..."

"How did you get in?" Both of us looked at her.

"I have a key."

"A key?" Jose questioned and she jumped off the counter. He almost had a heart attack.

"Yo, if you hurt my baby in your stomach I'ma fuck you up."

"Then stop acting like you don't know I have a key. You gave it to me." She busted out crying. He went over and hugged her but started grinning as he rested his chin on top of her head.

"You making me cry on purpose." She snatched away and stormed off. He blew his breath.

"Is this going to be how she acts for the entire pregnancy?"

"I'm afraid so bro."

"JOSEEEEEEEE! I'm still hungry." Now it was my turn to laugh.

"You better get your fiancé her food before she kills you." He snatched a water out the fridge and grabbed the plate.

"She can act spoiled all she wants as long as I can fuck whenever I want, I don't care." I rolled my eyes and waved him off. I really am happy he found someone. All I have to do now, is get petty ass Rakim on the same page and I know exactly what to do.

****

"What up Ced?" I heard his voice as I sat outside the office.

"Ummm, someone is here to see you."

121

"Whoever it is, tell them I'm busy."

"Nah, I think you'll wanna see this person." I stood up and made my way inside. He let a smile grace his face when he saw me.

"Still want me to send the person home?"

"Bye Ced and lock my door."

"For what?" He started laughing.

"I missed you ma." He stood and came over to where I was. It's been three days since we've spoken. I mean we text but we haven't heard each other's voice or seen one another.

"I missed you too but there's some things we need to discuss." I let my coat drop and heard him whisper damn. I had on a short dress where my ass damn near hung out and my tities did too. Granted the coat had me covered but I still felt like a ho.

"What's that?" He unzipped the back of my dress and slid his tongue in my mouth.

"What I tell you about wearing clothes that show all this?" He gripped my ass and I moaned out.

122

"I see you missed something else too." He unbuckled his jeans, kicked his sneakers off and everything else. He lifted me on the desk, spread my legs opened and dove straight in. This is not going as planned but I'm not mad either.

"I did but… Oh fuck!"

"Right there Rakim. Right there." I grinded all over his face and my legs shook as he sucked the life outta me. I literally had to lay back and catch my breath, which he gave me no time to do because he entered me quickly.

"I'll do whatever you want ma, just come home." It's funny because even though I had my own place with Jose, most of my stuff was at his and so were all the baby's things. We set the room up in neutral colors and have everything we needed there.

"Baby my back is hurting on this desk."

"Shit, hold on." He helped me up and led me to the small couch in the corner. Instead of sitting, I pushed him against the wall and stroked his man over and over. Both of us aggressively kissed each other and the second I felt a little pre-cum seep out. I kissed down his body and wrapped my lips around it. I wasn't on my knees and this position was killing me already but I continued.

"Jocelyn you're gonna make me. Ahhhhh got dammit." He came fast and down my throat.

"Turn around." He pressed me against the wall but not hard, entered me and had me moaning and scratching the side of his arms. There wasn't any music playing and if anyone was outside they probably heard.

"Throw it back ma." I did as he requested. Over the next hour or so we got reacquainted with one another and I loved it. Both of us knew once the baby came it would be a few weeks before we could have more sex so we tried to have it as much as possible.

"What's wrong? Why did you stop by?" He rubbed my hair out my face as we laid on the couch naked.

"Rakim if were gonna work, you have to stop tryna run Mari's life." He didn't say anything.

"Do you hear me?"

"Yea." I turned to look at him.

"Look baby. I know you're used to protecting and keeping her safe but she has a man to do it now. You know as well as I that Jose won't let anything happen to her."

"Why couldn't she find a safe nigga?" I laughed.

"You're not safe and I'm with you."

"Yea but you love me."

"And they love each other. Rakim let her breathe or she's gonna start hating you and you don't want that." He stared in the ceiling.

"Our babies are going to be first cousins so get used to seeing them together. And if you don't make yourself comfortable with it, then we can't be together."

"WHAT?" I grabbed my tight ass dress and started to put it back on.

"No one wants to see the two of you arguing all the time. And now with the kids coming we don't want them to think it's ok to hate one another and they're related."

"Me and your brother ain't related."

"He'll be your brother in law."

"Whatever."

"I'm serious Rakim. Get your shit together or no more pussy for you and I mean it."

"Fine!" I smiled and handed him his clothes.

"That's what I wanna hear. And just for agreeing, mami has something special planned for you tonight."

"Oh yea." He had a big ass grin on his face.

"Yup and I'm positive you're gonna love it." I looked online and found ways to surprise your man with a fantasy. I decorated the house already and couldn't wait for him to get home. Now if he hadn't agreed, I would've had to take it all down. What am I saying? His ass ain't have no choice.

Dashier

"How's it going soon to be brother in law?" Jose slowly walked in my office with papers in his hand. He had been out almost two months for the shooting and today was his first day returning.

"I can't complain, especially; with my fiancé helping me in more ways than one." I turned my face up and told him to get out.

"Ok. Ok." He always got a kick outta bringing up crazy shit between him and Mari. Let me mention another nigga taking her out though and he flips his damn lid.

"These papers need to be signed and I sent over an email about one of your personal accounts. Evidently, someone is removing funds outta one of them but only in small amounts."

"What you mean?" I pulled the email up and scanned it over.

"If you look right here." He went to point and I noticed pain on his face.

"You good?"

127

"Yea. Its gonna take a while for me to get all my strength back but I'm getting there."

"You need any medication?"

"Nah. I've been tryna deal with the pain because I don't wanna get hooked." I nodded.

"Here. You sit." I offered him the chair and stood.

"Thanks. You see here is a withdrawal for a thousand dollars. I usually don't mention it because it wasn't happening. But in the last couple of weeks, there's been one almost every other day and here's one for five thousand. Now I don't know if you're the one doing it but I can't keep your books straight if I have no clue why you're taking so much out." I turned the screen to me and checked the dates. Each one happened since Nika's been here.

"What's that?"

"I was gonna mention that next. Whoever is taking the money has been using an ATM card with her on it. What you see is the person using it in stores now. They must be using a fake ID."

"Hold on." I picked my phone up and called Levi.

"What's up bro?"

"You at work?"

"Yea."

"I'm gonna email you something. I need you to find out who it is and get back to me ASAP."

"You good?" He questioned.

"Nah, someone stealing from me."

"Send it now." I had Jose do it for me and once he confirmed he had it, I hung up.

"Dashier you're late on the conference call." Mari said walking in.

"Hey babe." She walked over and kissed him. One thing I can say about those two is n matter what goes on outside this company, they always remain professional.

"I'll see you later." Jose strolled out the office and closed the door behind him. Mari looked at me and could tell something wasn't right.

"Genesis."

"Yes, Ms. Davis." I heard her voice through the intercom and smiled on the inside.

Ever since the shit went down we haven't spoken, well;
we did when she picked Kingston up the day at my mom's.
She looked good as fuck and I wanted to hear her side but at
the time, we were dealing with Efrain. It's been a long time
and we needed to find out the truth behind his actions. Not that
I expected to hear what took place but I'm happy he vented.
My mom said, he's doing better and talking a lot more.

My pops got him a job and had him start in the
mailroom at one of the other banks. You would think Efrain be
pissed, however; he wasn't. My father always taught us you
have to work from the bottom to get to the top. I think it's why
everyone respected him and us so much. We didn't give out
favors to family members. I mean we did but not in a
noticeable way.

"Pick up line 1 and let them know Dashier and I ran
into an issue and we'll return the call later."

"Will do. Anything else?"

"No and do me a favor."

"Yes."

"Come to Mr. Davis office." I gave Mari a crazy ass look.

"Ummmm." You heard the hesitation in her voice.

"It's ok Genesis." She disconnected the call.

"You have to talk to her Dash."

"Mari, do I get involved with you and Jose?" She gave me the side eye.

"Whatever. You can't be inviting people in here without my permission."

"I can go." Genesis stood at the door in an all-black wrap around dress. Her hair was freshly done and I could tell she just had her nails done too.

"No, it's ok. I need for you two, to have the conversation because all this tension is making the office environment dry. No one wants to talk and everyone is afraid of Mr. Davis blowing up."

"Ms. Davis, I…"

"Regardless of how he spoke to you Genesis he won't hurt you." Mari walked to the door.

"He loves you Genesis." I heard her whisper and watched Mari close it behind her. I walked over to the mini bar, poured me a shot and let it burn going down. I had to deal with someone getting into my bank account and the fact that this woman is turning me on. I definitely need a drink.

"We can do this another time."

"Nah, its fine. I don't feel like hearing my sisters' mouth. Sit." I pointed to the chair.

"Mr. Davis, I didn't do the things Shanika and Manny accused me of and I'm sorry for not yelling it out downstairs. I was scared because he found me and would make me go back to Alabama with him. I wasn't being sneaky or anything, I was pretty much stuck and frozen with fear." I put my hands on the top of my head and leaned back in my seat as she finished speaking.

"I know what she did in the past has you skeptical and looking at me and everyone else crazy, but I'd never do that to you. I'm too scared to go to jail and I'm too scared to lose you. I lost you anyway but I still don't want to go to jail." I sat there

132

studying her body language and facial expressions and could tell she was sincere.

"I also want to thank you for allowing me to keep the place, car and being in Kingston's life, but I'm going to be moving this weekend. I dropped the car off to your place this morning." I sat up and let my arms lean on the desk.

"You didn't have to leave." She chuckled.

"You purchased that for me to please the courts. I don't think I should be living off your dime anymore, especially; when I have my own money. Now that I have a steady paycheck coming in, I can do it alone. I do appreciate it though." She stood to leave and I rose to my feet as well.

"I appreciate you letting me tell my side and not yelling or kicking me out. I hope one day we can be friends but I understand if it's not what you want. Have a good day."

"Genesis." She turned to me. My words were stuck in my throat.

"Are you ok?" I cleared my throat.

"Yea. Ummm, thanks for telling me." She smiled and left me standing there stuck on stupid. I wanted to run after her or call her back but Maxine coming in, stopped me.

"Mr. Davis can we discuss Ms. Tyler, Rogers or whatever her name is?"

"Excuse me." I returned to sit at my desk.

"The woman who recently stepped out has two names and a bad attitude. I had to write her up not too long ago for being disrespectful in the office."

"You're not her supervisor, so how did you write her up?"

"I know and I apologize but no one was here and I felt it had to be done." I looked at her crazy.

"What did she do?" I started looking on my computer.

"Well, I asked for her ID card the day we found out she attempted to rob you and she cursed me out. Then, told me I better not speak to her again. Frankly, she's a time bomb ticking and her negativity isn't good for this office." I rested my chin on my hands and stared at this petty ass woman.

She tried extremely hard not to say anything racist but I read between the lines and so far she called Genesis, hood, ratchet, and ghetto all in one sentence. Never mind the fact she mentioned the so-called robbery attempt.

"Maxine you know better than to approach me with nonsense. Why didn't you take this down to HR?" I went back to the email I was reading.

"I figured you should know I put a request in for her to be terminated." I peeked from around my computer. This bitch doesn't even have the authority to fire anyone. I pressed the intercom on my phone and called my sister.

"How can I help you Mr. Davis?" Mari spoke on the speaker.

"Ms. Davis can you and your secretary come into my office?"

"We'll be right there." Maxine had a look of nervousness on her face and I loved it. I'm not even sure I'd stop Genesis if she hooked off. My sister knocked and the two of them stepped in.

"Is something wrong?"

"Ms. Davis, are you aware that your secretary goes by two last names?" Mari stared straight at Maxine.

"Yes." I was a tad bit shocked because I didn't know, or maybe she told me and I didn't care.

"Since it's been brought up for some reason, my secretary uses her father's last name for? Matter of fact, I'll disclose that information to you at a later time. What is this about?"

"Maxine here, unbeknownst to me wrote your secretary up for being insubordinate, hostile and disrespectful. Isn't that about right?" I stared at Maxine who gave a fake smile.

"Yes, I did. Ms. Davis you weren't here and Ms. Tyler, Rogers or whatever her name is started cursing in the workplace and threatening to fight me. You know we don't tolerate things like that here." Genesis was turning red and I saw hate on her face. I stood and sat on the edge of my desk because I have no doubt she's about to lose it.

"Maxine, I thought we discussed previously you starting unnecessary drama." She put her head down.

136

"And if I'm correct, didn't you attempt to take her ID badge even though Mr. Davis told her he was excusing everyone for the day, and she could return? And the fact you're still very jealous of her speaking with Mr. Davis?"

"I... I..."

"You told my secretary the boss is off limits and the only person he'd sleep with is you." I snapped my neck to look at her.

"I don't recall saying those things to her."

"What is your problem with my secretary? She doesn't work with him, or spend any time in his office. Nor does he call her for anything. If I had to speculate, I'd say you were obsessed over your boss."

"Never. I have a man."

"Genesis do you deny anything Maxine is saying?" She stood and so did I. Mari had a smirk on her face.

"Maxine, I told you not to try me, didn't I." Genesis said it in a firm tone.

"Do you see how hostile's she's getting now? I mean it isn't even necessary."

"Maxine she only asked you a question." I told her and Maxine looked shook.

"Let me be clear on one thing with you." Genesis was in front of me and I can't front. Her ass was touching my leg and all I wanted to do is grab it.

"Mr. Davis and I are not a couple, nor do we have sex. If we did it's none of your business and as far as you writing me up, I've already filed a grievance about you."

"Excuse me." Maxine now stood.

"You walk around here pretending to be better than the rest of the woman in this office and have no problem putting them down."

"I don't know what you're speaking of."

"Come to find out, all you are is Mr. Davis secretary. You have no authority to write me or anyone else up. Better yet, no right to try and have me fired."

"Fired?" Mari questioned because this was news to her.

"Yea, I went down and spoke to your sister and I think she and I are on the same page now, especially; after finding out she's been doing things you asked even though they were unethical."

"What are you talking about?" I asked.

"Maxine here, has been trying to get everyone who she thinks is a threat; fired. The crazy part is, she has no idea I can be a bitch who will not only beat her ass but make sure she never works as a secretary anywhere." Maxine backed up into a wall as Genesis stood in her face.

"You got one more time and I'll make sure everyone knows your little secret."

"Ok Genesis." I grabbed her waist and pulled her away.

"I'm not about to let your jealous ass get me fired. Keep fucking with me bitch." I turned and Mari was sitting at my desk tryna hold her laugh in.

"Mr. Davis, this is inappropriate and…"

"What's inappropriate is you trying to get staff fired, harassing them on a daily basis and getting your sister, who will be terminated for her part in your foolery, mixed up in it. What type of game were you playing?" She began pacing my office.

"Dashier, you know how much I love you and you constantly allow these little sluts to work here. You think I want to see them every day trying to get your attention? How could you disrespect me like that?" On the outside looking in, one would think I fucked her but never.

"Bitch, are you crazy. He's taken." Genesis shouted, jumped outta my arms and started beating the fuck outta Maxine. She was no match and looked half dead by the time I pulled Genesis off.

"Mari, this shit ain't funny. Take Genesis outta here." She didn't even budge.

"What the fuck going on?" Jose shouted. He looked at Maxine on the ground, then at Genesis, then Mari.

"I want my money Jose."

"WHAT?"

"Yea, I told him it's only a matter of time before Genesis digs in her ass. He said, it wouldn't happen."

"GET OUT!" I was mad as hell at her. Security came running in and both of them were grinning. It's no secret Maxine was hated by everyone.

"Take her outta here and make sure you get her badge and anything else belonging to the company. She no longer works here." When they got her up and out my office, I slammed the newly fixed door and stared at Genesis who was pacing and rubbing her temples.

"Genesis."

"Don't say anything right now. I told you the bitch wanted you and she was testing me."

"But we're not together and…" She stopped and came closer to me.

"I don't care what you say Dashier Davis. You know as well as I, that we'll never be over." I smirked and walked to my desk.

"Don't get it fucked up though. I know you still love me and vice versa but the way you treated me has not been forgiven."

"Who said we won't ever be over?" Why did I ask that? She came over and opened her dress. The panty set she had on was sexy and I wanted to snatch it all off.

"The way your dick responds to me and how your heart beats, tells me." She had her hand on my chest.

"I miss you too baby." She straddled me and pressed her lips to mine. I should've stopped her but I couldn't.

"Fuck Genesis." She undid the bra and let me suck on her breasts. My dick was brick hard and fighting to get outta my clothes and into her. Outta nowhere she stopped, put her clothes back on and stood.

"Tha fuck you doing?" I was staring at her.

"You have to work for me to come back." I snatched her arm and slammed her on the desk.

"Don't play fucking games with me." I unbuckled my jeans and let the tip of my dick slid up and down the middle of her pussy. Her clit was pulsating and I could see the urge for her to release.

KNOCK! KNOCK! I hurried to fix myself and pulled Genesis off the desk. I had her run in the bathroom to get herself together."

"No need to run Genesis. No office sex huh?" Jose got a kick outta this.

"What?" I sat down before he got to see how hard I was.

"I'd rather stay here because it's no telling what I'm gonna see. I wanted to tell you Levi has been calling and said to open your email." He closed the door back and Genesis stepped out the bathroom and went to her desk looking unbothered.

I opened the email and if I didn't hate her before, I definitely hate her now. I closed my computer down, locked my door and left for the day. I need to gather my thoughts because I'm about to kill this bitch.

Genesis

"Dash you scared me." I closed the door to my new two-bedroom apartment and placed my keys and purse on the counter. He was sitting in my living room with no T.V. on.

"Do you love me Genesis? I mean really love me?" He had both of his hands together as if he were praying as he stared at me.

"I'm in love with you Dash and how did you get into my place?" He sat there and never said a word. Instead of waiting for an answer, I went in my bedroom, removed my clothes and hopped in the shower. I didn't expect him to join me and I'm glad he chose not to because as horny as I am, I'd probably throw the pussy at him.

I dried off with the towel, opened the bedroom door and found him lying in my bed. Granted, it's not the huge California King he has but its mine. And why is he here anyway? I thought about questioning him and changed my mind because he'd probably tell me not to worry about it, or he can do what he wanted.

As I pulled some clothes out of my dresser, I couldn't help but feel his watchful eyes on me. I turned around and saw the affectionate look he gave me and it made my heart skip a beat. I may be horny and I am going to try my best not to give in but I'm not sure I can hold out.

I mean over the last week and a half, he's sent me text messages telling me how much he's missed me, sent flowers to the job under an alias and even ordered lunch for me, through Mari. Each time I received something I wanted to send my thanks but his sister told me not to. She said and I quote, *He treated you like shit, didn't wanna hear anything you had to say when you wanted to explain and told you to stay away from him. Make his ass sweat.* I definitely found it funny for her to be on my side.

"Come here Genesis." He called in a demanding tone.

"I'm fine right here." He chuckled and moved the sheet off his legs and revealed his naked body. Call me all the freaks you want but my mouth watered at the sight if his semi erect dick.

"Oh you want some of this?" He began stroking it slow. I licked my lips and our eyes met.

"I came here because my dick was calling out for you, but if you don't want me, I can go." He stopped stroking himself and went to stand. I let him and fell back on the bed. My head was at the edge with his dick in my face.

"You sure this is what you want?" He was now standing over me with his dick touching my lips. I didn't bother answering him and swallowed him whole. He used his hands to lean over and circle my clit that grew instantly.

"Mmmm hmmm. I knew you missed this dick." I was slobbing, sucking, jerking, juggling his balls and licking that sensitive part under. His body began shaking, which let me know he's about to cum.

"Cum all over my body Dash." And just like that, he pulled out and his cum was on my tities, stomach and at the top of my pussy.

"Got damn, I needed that. Come here." He yanked me up by the hair, wrapped his hand around it and forced his tongue in my mouth.

"Get off me." I pushed him away, turned around and bent down on the bed touching my ankles.

"Eat my pussy and you better do it real good or you won't be feeling the inside of these walls until you do." I could see the smile gracing his face as he smacked my ass a few times and went head first.

"Ahhh shit baby. It feels so fucking goooooood. I'm about to cum and you better lick it up. I wanna taste my pussy in your mouth when we kiss." His finger went in my ass at the same time he sucked on my nub. I screamed so loud and collapsed on the bed.

"Now taste this good ass pussy." He turned me around and threw his tongue down my throat again. We were so engaged in the kiss, I didn't realize I had tears coming down my eyes until he wiped them.

"I'm sorry Genesis. I swear, I'll never treat you that way again."

"FUCK!!!!!!" I shouted when he entered me and laid me down gently on the bed.

"Are you pregnant?"

147

"No. I took the pill like you asked." He nodded and slowly moved in and outta me.

"You will be before tonight is over."

"Dash."

"I love you Genesis." We started kissing again and by the time we finished, he came in me at least three times and the sun had come up. Ain't no way in hell I'm going to work today. Fuck it! The boss said I don't have to. He pulled me closer, rested his hand across my body and fell asleep. I could live like this forever with him.

****

"Seems like you two made up." Demaris said and pointed to a hickey on my neck.

"What makes you think he did this?" She stopped walking and turned.

"As if your love-struck ass would be standing here alive if you allowed someone else to touch you."

"Whatever." I waved her off and she stepped in her office.

"Ms. Rogers, can you come in my office?" Dashier spoke over the speaker. It was weird for him to be calling me in there. I took the short walk across the office and stepped in. He asked me to close the door and sat back in his seat.

"Yes."

"First off, don't think giving me head this morning and no pussy is ok."

"Huh?"

"I don't care how sore your pussy is. If you can't give me both, don't tease me with one."

"Yes sir."

"Second, I'm gonna fuck the shit outta you later and I can't wait."

"Dash you know I'm sore." He gestured for me to come to him.

"You like this." His hand went under my skirt, he let his fingers dip in my wetness and twirl around inside. I almost fell when my knees became weak.

"Yessssss. Oh God, yessssss."

"Then cum for me before my new secretary comes in."

149

"Dash."

"Hurry up. The person will be walking in, in one minute. Show your man he can make you cum fast." I leaned over and placed my mouth on his.

"Damn, you're about to cum." I nodded with our lips still attached.

"How's it feel baby?" I released and my clit was super sensitive.

"I love you so much Dash." I put my head in the crook of his neck and inhaled his cologne.

"I know and I feel the same. You taste good too baby." He sucked my juices off, smacked my ass and had me go in the bathroom to clean up.

"Mr. Davis, I'm here. Where do I start?"

"George?" I popped my head out the bathroom.

"Really? You could've told me y'all were in here fucking."

"We weren't." I gave him a fake smile and he rolled his eyes.

"Today anyway."

"TMI Dash. TMI! Now if I'm gonna be your new secretary I need to lay down some ground rules with these heffas." I heard Dash cracking up.

"And what's that?"

"First off, the only women who need to be in this office are Genesis and my sister in law. Two... if any of these bitches even try and step to my husband, I'm whooping their ass, female or not and third. Where's my desk? I need to tidy it up and get myself acquainted with it."

"Acquainted with it?" I was confused.

"Yea, you know put my photos up, mints on the desk for the bitches with bad breath, things like that." Dash shook his head and I was hysterical laughing as he walked out talking shit.

"Why is George your secretary? I thought he had a job." He stood and walked with me to the door.

"He was working with his mother and stopped after the shit in the hospital. Levi said, he's been bored and since I know my woman will most likely beat up any chick I hire, he's the best we got."

"Long as you know." I pecked his lips and stepped out.

"Bitch, let me know when and where y'all fuck. I don't wanna smell the sex in the air or sit on whatever y'all fucked on." He whispered but I heard him.

"No sex in the office George." Mari said.

"Say the woman who fucks her man at least once a week in his."

"You talk too much."

"But you know this and continue telling me stuff. Love you too now bye. I have to start my day." He shooed us away and I was impressed because throughout the day, he answered phones, had the tech guy update him on the computer software and even made sure all Dash's appointments were set up for tomorrow. He was on point for it to be his first day. Me, him and Mari ended up having lunch together and even invited the other women to join us. They were cool when we went out and I think we should all get to no one another anyway.

"Move in with me." Dash blurted out on the way to our cars. I had the Mercedes fixed he purchased for me that Manny's childish ass destroyed and returned it. I loved it but I

152

also didn't want him assuming he had to take care of me. I ended up getting a 2017 Toyota Camry. It was very nice and I loved the gadgets inside.

"I just got that place and believe it or not, I like it." He pulled me closer.

"And I like you, plus I don't trust Nika and Manny. They're around and until I find them, I wanna always know you're safe."

"Dashhhhhhhh."

"You know you wanna wake up to my sexy ass everyday." I smiled.

"What if they lie again and you kick me out? I don't wanna take the chance of..." He cut me off by kissing me.

"I'll never do that again and I'll apologize a million times if you want. I was confused and when the nigga said y'all were still a couple it pissed me off. I wanna keep you in me and Kingston's life. And my sperm is pretty potent so I'm sure you're already pregnant. What do you say?" He placed kisses on the side of my neck.

"How can I say no to that?"

153

"You better or I'll kill him right here." I looked and saw Manny with a gun to Dash's head and went into panic mode, where Dash was very calm.

"If you don't remove the gun from the back of my head, you won't live to see another day." The gun cocked.

"Move back Genesis."

"No." I pushed him out the way and stood in front of Manny.

"Let's go Manny. I'm tired of you bothering him." I was scared as hell but I couldn't let him hurt Dash over me.

"Hell no Genesis." I put my hand out to stop him from moving any closer.

"I'll be fine Dash. He won't hurt me."

"No, but I will." I can't even tell you what I was hit with because the blackness took over instantly.

Shanika

"How's it feel to see the woman you fell in love with out for the count?" Manny had Genesis in his arms as he walked to the car. Me, I had the same gun pointed at him, I just knocked her over the head with.

"Its gonna feel better when I strangle you with my own hands." He smiled and for some reason it sent chills down my spine.

"Tha fuck going on out here?" That fine Spanish man asked and hit the alarm on his truck.

"Ain't you the same bitch my fiancé beat up?"

"Fiancé?" I questioned walking backwards to the car.

"Damn right fiancé. Yo, is that Genesis he putting in the car and is she bleeding?" He went to move forward and Dash stopped him.

"She's fine."

"Jose my feet hurt and…" Mari came out and he instantly placed her behind him. She wasn't huge but I noticed her stomach poking out.

"Hurry the fuck up Nika. We gotta get outta here."
Manny shouted and I heard the car start. I used my hand to feel
behind me and opened the passenger side door.

"Since you're so worried about her, I'll return her when
you pay me."

"Pay you. Bitch ain't nobody paying you for shit." I
heard Mari's voice but that nigga kept her covered. I hopped in
the car and Manny peeled out the parking lot.

BOOM! BOOM! Bullets were hitting the car but it
didn't matter because we got away.

"YES! We're about to be rich off this bitch." I looked
in the back seat and Genesis had blood leaking down her face
and a knot forming. She looked unconscious too.

"How are we gonna get her in the hotel room?"

"What the fuck you mean? She's gonna wake up and
walk." I leaned back in the seat and relaxed as we took the long
ride to Connecticut.

Its where we've been holed up thinking of a plan to get
Kingston. Unfortunately, we couldn't get anywhere near him
but we got the next best thing, which is Genesis. I saw the

same love and adoration in his eyes for her, he used to have for me but something was different. He not only loved her but was in love with her and she felt the same. How in the hell did those two get caught up in just a short time? I'm not saying it can't happen but they wasted no time for two people who recently met.

I remember when he loved me that way. He catered to my every want and need. Made love to me any and everywhere and nothing was too much money when it came to me. He spared no expense and I loved it. I just wanted more and my greedy ways got me caught, however; she will be my meal ticket. It's the least he can do since he won't allow me to see my son. Not that I really care because there's no bond but it's the principle.

We pulled up to the 5-star hotel, parked in the back and got out. I didn't think we'd be able to stay in a place like this until Manny had one of his friends from home, hack into one of Dash's bank accounts and steal money here and there. He told us to withdraw money as much as possible because if anyone finds out, the account will be frozen and sure enough, the last time we tried to take more money, the ATM kept the debit card.

I had Manny ask if he could get into any other accounts of his and the guy said no. Dash had extra security on his big money accounts. The only way he was able to get into this one is because it had someone else linked to it and guess who the person is? Yup, his precious Genesis. I was pissed to see this nigga gave her a few million. Four to be exact. I guess a million for each year she had Kingston.

"Get up." He smacked Genesis in the face a few times. She eventually opened her eyes and stared at us. You could tell she had no idea where she was.

"Where am I?" She held her head with her hand and glanced around.

"In Connecticut. We're about to use you for ransom."

"Ransom?"

"Yup. I think Dash would pay good money to have you returned safe."

"Get the fuck out the car." She let one foot hit the ground and I cocked the gun.

158

"If you even think about screaming, I'm gonna blow your got damn head off." She rolled her eyes and didn't make a sound. Manny ran around the front and opened the side door. Thank goodness no one was in the hallway because she definitely looked fucked up in the face.

"Why are you doing this?"

"Let's see. My cousin is fucking my ex, keeping my son away and somehow the judge got wind of me robbing banks and won't allow me within 50ft of Kingston."

"You think he should?" Manny unlocked the room door and pushed her in.

"Manny are you seriously going along with this? I know we've been through some things but this isn't you." He slammed her against the wall and crashed his lips on hers.

"What the hell are you doing?" She pushed him off and he began ripping her shirt. She started fighting him and he smacked the heck outta her. Once she hit the floor he started unbuckling his jeans. I give it to Genesis, she wasn't giving up without a fight.

"Hell to the no Manny." I had to step in because regardless of what's going on, no woman deserves to go through that.

"What?"

"You ain't raping nobody."

"She my girl so basically I'm not raping her."

"Nigga, she ain't your girl and she's fighting and telling you no, so yea its rape." He stood and backed away.

"I'm sorry Genesis. I miss you and you promised you were coming back." He had his head in his hands; meanwhile Genesis was hysterical crying with her knees to her chest.

"Please let me go." For an ounce of a second I felt bad but then my common sense kicked in and I told her to shut the fuck up.

"Call him."

"No."

"You don't have a choice." I put the gun under her chin and she nodded. I passed her the cell and watched her dial his number with ease. Who the hell remembers phone numbers these days? I put him on speaker and waited for him to answer.

"Tell me you're ok Genesis." You could hear panic in his voice. How the hell did he even know it was her?

"He tried to rape me Dash." The phone got quiet and all of a sudden there was a loud crash.

"Let her go Nika. It's me you want."

"I thought about it Dash and if I let her go, then I lose out. Therefore; I think I'll keep her."

"What do you want?"

"Well, since you asked. I want five million dollars and don't say you don't have it because you put four in this bitch bank account."

"Dash don't give it to her. I'll be fine."

WHAP! WHAP! Manny smacked fire from her ass.

"YOOOOOO! Leave her the fuck alone."

"You have 10 hours to get the money to a location I'm gonna send to your phone and don't think I'm stupid. I know all about the people you know on the force and all the tricks that cops and detectives do to lure you in. See, I'm gonna leave her with Manny while I come get the money and one call from me and your precious Genesis will have her innocence taken."

161

"Let me see that's she's ok. Facetime me." He hung up and I called him back.

"Why are her clothes ripped? And what the fuck happened to her face?" I turned the camera back to me.

"You heard her say he tried to rape her and she needed her face smacked a few times."

"Manny, you can't be that desperate but I got a trick for your ass."

"What's that supposed to mean?" He smiled and I saw Rakim behind him with a huge iPad.

"You went after my girl and now your parents, two sisters and brothers will suffer if anything happens to her." I looked at they were all tied up in a room with gasoline cans around them. Some guy was covered with one of those flame lighters you use to set fire on the grill.

"Yo! You better not touch my family."

"Seems like we both have bargaining chips. You see Manny, you messed around and picked the wrong nigga to fuck with. Nika should've filled you in on the Davis family. Oh and Nika, your mom is a little pissed you got her killed."

162

Manny was fuming and I had a little remorse for my mother but not a lot. She kept calling me stupid for trying to go after Dash, so oh well.

"And just so you know, every hour that passes and my girl ain't here, one of them will be set on fire." He hung up and Manny threw the lamp across the room.

"Take her back."

"What? Hell no!" He yoked me up by the shirt.

"Bitch, I'm not about to lose my family over her."

"Too bad. This is what you wanted so now we're following through." He started pacing back and forth.

"I'll be back."

"He's gonna kill you Nika." Genesis whispered laying on the floor in a fetal position. One of her eyes were shut. Her lip was busted and the knot on her forehead still had blood coming out.

"Who?"

"Manny will if anything happens to his family and Dash will, if anything happens to me."

"You think you're perfect, don't you?" She wiped her eyes and sat up the best she could. I noticed how dizzy she was.

"I never wanted to fall for him Nika. Trust me, we both tried to avoid it but being around one another everyday it happened."

"Yea right. This was revenge for you."

"Nika, I didn't care you slept with those boys. I mean yes, I was upset but you were always in competition with me for some reason. All I ever did was try and be your sister because we were all we got but you were jealous of me and I don't know why."

"I wasn't jealous, just didn't understand why all the boys wanted you. I was pretty too and..."

"Nika you were very pretty and believe it or not, I was most of their second choices because they wanted you. Then, you started sleeping with them and became a totally different person. You made me feel like shit because I wasn't having sex. You talked about me like a dog, told everyone I was a whore and the list goes on and on." I sat against the wall listening to her take us back in time and she was right.

I did and said horrible things about her when we were young. There was no specific reason as to why, I just did. Neither of us said anything else and I noticed her other eye closing. She ended up falling asleep and so did I. It wasn't until I heard a loud noise outside the door that I woke up to my worst nightmare.

"She's going to be fine son." My mom rubbed my shoulders when I hung up on Nika. When the number popped up, I knew it was Genesis because most kidnappers make them call for a ransom. Hell yea, I knew Nika wanted money. After Levi sent me the email not too long ago showing me Nika at the ATM's and banks taking the money out, I knew it wouldn't be long before she requested more. I didn't know it would be at the expense of Genesis.

"Ma, did you see her face and the nigga tried to rape her." I threw everything off the kitchen counter.

I went to my parents' house because my brother was there. I knew if anyone was down to help, he would. Not that the other two weren't but I tried to keep them out of it. Especially Efrain. He had a lot going on and I didn't wanna stress him out. Shit we still can't find Gavin or the other guys who violated him.

"Dash there's someone on the phone for you." Mari brought it over to me. It seemed like everyone came to help.

"Who this?"

166

"Is this Dash?"

"Who the fuck is this?" I looked down at the phone and noticed it was an unknown number.

"Look, I remembered your number from Nika dialing it."

"Manny?" I questioned and everyone stopped.

"Yea. Listen, I'll tell you where she is if you let my family go."

"How do I know you're not lying?"

"I admit, I came up here to reclaim my woman but you stole her heart and as bad as I don't wanna say it, she is in love with you. Shit, I don't think she ever loved me the same." I stood there listening to him vent about losing Genesis, hoping it would make him give me the address.

"It hurts like hell knowing she wants another man but I have to take the L because my family comes first." Levi put his thumb up to let me know he traced the call. Rakim got on the phone with his people to try and locate him.

"Where is she and is she ok?" He blew his breath and I instantly thought the worst.

"We're in Connecticut at one of the Hiltons around the airport. You should probably hurry up and get here because that hit to her forehead Nika gave her is bad."

"Call an ambulance for her." He didn't respond

"The room number is 405." He hung the phone up and I heard Rakim telling someone to hurry up and get there but not to touch him. He needed to keep an eye on him so we can make sure he wasn't lying. I had Raphael's people keep Manny's family where they were until further notice.

"I'm coming." Mari said and tried to walk out with me.

"Are you crazy? I do not feel like hearing that nigga's mouth and you're pregnant. Mari it's too far of a ride."

"Mommy." I picked my phone up and called Jose.

"You find her?" He asked.

"Yea, hopefully. Look, we're about to ride out and Mari wanted to come. I know you're doing something in regards to Dutchess but I can't take her."

"She ain't going. I'ma about to hit her phone. Be safe and I'll see y'all when you get back." I heard Mari's phone

168

ring and had George take her inside. Once he did, Rakim and Levi jumped in the truck with me.

The entire drive to Connecticut all I could think about was Genesis. I wanted to hear her voice and see with my own eyes she was ok. It's funny how in this last year of meeting her and my son, we've become closer than Nika and I ever were. We talked about everything and if I mentioned going outta town, she had no problem tagging along or even volunteering to go. I think it was more because she said, she's only been to Alabama and would love to travel but who cares? I couldn't get her cousin to go anywhere.

I admit when Nika and Manny yelled the shit out at the bank about her tryna rob me, I behaved stupid. I was hurt and didn't wanna believe another woman could do me the same. It took my mother talking to me the day she picked Kingston up. She said, *Dashier that woman loves you and you're treating her wrong. And don't forget she told us, she'd never rob a bank because she's scared of guns and scared of going to jail.* I went home that night and thought about what she said and agreed. I may have been blinded my Nika, but everything about Genesis said she wasn't like that. I had to get outta my own way and push my pride aside to see it.

"There it is." Rakim pointed to the hotel Manny said they were at. I can't even tell you how we got here in two hours, when it usually takes three. I jumped out and ran past the front desk and to the stairs. Fuck an elevator it would take too long.

"Call an ambulance right now and tell them to come up to 405." I heard Levi yell out. I hoped Manny called one for her but since he never mentioned it, I bet she's still here.

"Please be ok. Please be ok." I said running down the hall to find her. When we got to the door I didn't give two fucks about paying for it. I kicked the shit open and dropped in front of Genesis when I saw her. She was barely breathing and she looked worse up close than in the facetime.

"Genesis wake up baby. I'm here." I lifted her and placed her on the bed. I wrapped a sheet around her because the nigga tore her clothes.

"Let me go." I didn't have to look, to know Rakim had

Nika. She was shouting but it's no telling what he did to shut

her up.

"Dash it hurts." I heard Genesis whisper.

"What hurts? Tell me where the pain is?"

"My head is pounding really bad." Her nose started

bleeding and her eyes were rolling. I didn't have time to panic

because the paramedics pushed me to the side and rushed her

out.

"Let's go bro." Levi led me out the door and down the

steps. We met the paramedics outside and followed them to the

hospital.

"Yea." I answered my phone through Bluetooth for

Rakim.

"She'll be in Jersey when you're done."

"Thanks, and I'll call as soon as I know something."

"A'ight." We hung up and I called to tell my mother

what was going on. I knew she'd inform Mari and George who

were still there helping her with Kingston.

We pulled in behind the ambulance and I watched as they carted Genesis away. I called her parents and told them I'd have my sister book them on the next flight out. I fell back in the chair and prayed she was gonna be ok.

****

"Dash." I heard a light whisper and looked up to see Genesis smiling down. She had been asleep for a day. Sadly, the hit to her head caused a concussion and a small aneurism on her brain. They had to do a small operation to get it. The swelling is going down on her eye and the doctor said she would have headaches for a while, otherwise; she's ok.

"I'm here." I grabbed her hand and kissed the top of it.

"Where's Kingston? Is he ok?"

"He's fine and so is this one." I pointed to her stomach that had monitors on it.

"Dash."

"You lied about taking the plan b pill but I understand." I turned the volume up on the machine so she could hear the heartbeat. I knew she felt different when we made up but she said no when I asked and I left it alone.

"I deserved for you to keep it from me after the way I treated you. I'm glad you didn't lose it." She started crying.

"I thought they were going to kill me and then Manny ripped my clothes off and tried to…"

"Shhhhh. No need to dwell on it anymore. I promise they will never get to you again."

"But…"

"No need to ask a question you already know the answer to." She nodded and poked her lips out for a kiss.

"You are so lucky I love you because right now your breaths is.-" She covered her mouth and started laughing. I moved her hand and pecked her lips.

Over the next two days, the doctor kept her in the hospital and I stayed with her until it was time to go home. I did run out to one of the malls when she fell asleep to grab a few things to put on. I got her an outfit to wear home too because I tossed the clothes she had on and she ain't going home in the hospital gown.

"You know you're moving in with me." I told her on the drive back to Jersey.

"I wouldn't have it any other way." I parked in front of the house, help her in, stayed as she took a shower and left. I had unfinished business with this bitch and its already been a few days too long that she's still been allowed to breathe. I pulled in the warehouse and saw Rakim rushing out.

"What's up?"

"Jocelyn is in labor."

"Wait! She's only eight and a half months."

"I know. Come to the hospital when you're done." I sent a text to Jose and Mari to let them know I'm in town. Both of them were on their way to the hospital with Jocelyn. Evidently, they were out eating and she had contractions. I can't wait until that's Genesis. I missed out on Kingston, but I won't miss out on this one.

"I'm not even going to waste my breath on you. Have fun in hell." I pointed my gun at them.

"But I told you where she was." Manny cried out.

"And I said, I wouldn't kill your family. They're still alive but you won't be." I shot both her and Manny in the head and watched their bodies drop. My girl needed me and the longer I was here, the longer I was away.

I stopped by the hospital on the way and both of my parents were there ,and so were Efrain and Geri, Jose and Mari and Levi and George. I asked where Rakim was and they said in the back.

A few Spanish dudes walked in and Jose introduced them as his best friends and a few cousins. The waiting room was packed. I thought about calling Genesis but she had to rest. I sent her a text and sat there waiting with everyone else for Jocelyn to deliver my niece or nephew.

Jocelyn

"It hurts so bad Rakim." I reached out for his hand when he walked in the room.

I was out eating with Jose and Mari when I felt some pain and ignored it. The doctor said there may be some Braxton hicks here and there. They weren't as bad until I finished eating. I assumed acid reflux and ignored it until I stood to use the bathroom and felt water dripping down my leg.

Mari was so excited, Jose had to stop her from jumping up and down. He held my hand and walked with me to the truck. I thought it would be fine but once the contraction hit after my water broke, I was in extreme pain. It felt like someone was inside my stomach twisting my intestines.

When we got in the truck Mari was already on the phone telling Rakim to meet us at the hospital. Next, she called her parents and I can't tell you what happened after that because I had to grip the door handle to fight through the pain. If you never had a child, you don't know what I'm talking about but these pains are excruciating.

Jose sped to the hospital and both him and Mari came in the room with me. The nurse sent my brother in the hallway and she stayed in to help me undress. He came back in smiling and kissed my cheek. I told him he was next and of course, he rubbed Mari's belly.

I wanted them to stay with me during the birthing process but they both declined and said Rakim should be in here. I wasn't going to keep him out and only asked because I was scared and wanted more people with me.

"You good ma. How far are the contractions?" The nurse and I both smiled when he asked. I had him watching baby channels with me but who knew he actually paid attention?

"The doctor said, I'm at five right now. I have to get to ten and can't get an epidural until then."

"A'ight. You need anything?" He sat on the bed facing me.

"I need for you and Jose to put your pride aside and be cordial."

"Not the time for this Jocelyn."

177

"Why nottttttttttt?" I squeezed his hand hard as a contraction ripped through me.

"Concentrate on having my baby and we'll talk later." I nodded and he jumped off the bed.

"You're bleeding. Yooooo get a doctor in here." I looked and there was blood coming from down below. I started panicking and asked him to get my brother.

"What's wrong?"

"Jose, I don't think the baby is going to make it." I cried as the doctor walked in.

"Why? What happened doc?" He held my hand and watched the doctor re-check me.

"We have to hurry and deliver the baby. The cord is wrapped around the neck and you're bleeding because somehow you're already ten centimeters. Did you start pushing?"

"No. I don't think so. Ahhhhhhhh!" I screamed and watched the nurses and doctors rushing to prepare.

"I'll be outside Jocelyn."

"What if?" He kissed my forehead.

"There is no what if Jocelyn. Mommy is watching and she's not going to let anything go wrong. Stop panicking."

"Ok. Ok. Is it ok if Rakim's mom comes in? Do you think its wronggggggggg? Oh my Godddddddd it hurts."

"Can she get an epidural or something?" Rakim barked.

"It's too late. When you feel the next one push as hard as you can Ms. Alvarado. We have to get this baby out."

"I'll send her in." A few seconds later his mom came running in. She grabbed my hand and started rubbing my hair.

"Jocelyn, I know it hurts honey but you have to try and relax. You're putting stress on the baby and the doctor has to get him or her out."

"I can see the top of the head." Rakim shouted.

"One more push Ms. Alvarado."

"Make sure you push with all your might ok?"

"Here comes another one." I squeezed her hand tight, pushed and felt a release on my lower half.

"Nurse bring me the crib." His mom wiped my forehead and let my hand go.

"Come on lil man. I need you to cry." I heard Rakim say and started crying myself. He had a few tears coming down his face too.

"Come on. Come on." I heard the doctor saying.

"Is my baby ok?" The room fell silent and I started breathing fast.

WAAAA! WAAA! I heard the cry and looked up to the ceiling and thanked my mom and God for letting him live.

"Take him to NICU right away." I saw the nurse pushing him out and Rakim was directly behind her.

"I'll be back. Ma, keep an eye on her please. Jose go check on Jocelyn." I heard him yell out the door.

"Wait Jose! They're cleaning her up." I heard Mari yell when she stepped in.

"Is she ok? Is my sister ok?" Mari looked over at me and I nodded.

"Yes. She's ok." Mari went over to him at the door and I could hear her saying she's fine and give them a minute. The doctor told me he had to give me a few stitches due to the tear. After he finished, the nurse had me stand for a few seconds and placed me in a wheelchair. She said, they were putting me in a different room because this is only the birthing one and moms don't stay in here anymore. She literally pushed me to the other side of the floor, which is stupid. Why didn't they let me stay in the same one? They didn't even give me time to get myself together.

"Are yo ok?" Mari asked and her mom was brushing my hair back.

"I was so scared. He wasn't breathing and it took a few seconds for him to cry. I thought my baby died." I saw both of them crying.

"He's an Alvarado and Davis. We're strong and he's going to be fine. I can't wait to hold him."

"They took him out. Do you think he's ok?" I felt myself getting worked up again.

"Jocelyn, they took him out because the cord was wrapped around his throat. They need to make sure his oxygen level is good. Also, they'll weigh him and make sure he's good to come meet you. Like Mari said, he's an Alvarado and Davis.

I have faith that my grandson will be fine and I said a prayer to your mom too." I looked at her.

"What? She may not be here physically, but she is spiritually and I'm positive her and God made sure he was ok."

"Thank you for that." Jose said coming in and gave her a hug.

"Mari let's give them a minute."

"What if they bring my nephew back?"

"Girl, get your ass out here."

"I'm sorry baby, I know y'all need a minute but I'm coming back when my nephew comes in so hurry up." We all laughed and she kissed Jose on the way out.

"You did it sis. You had a damn baby." He sat next to me and I rested my head on his shoulder.

"I thought he…" He cut me off and told me not to even speak on it.

"My nephew is here and healthy. Did you get to see him?"

"No. They rushed him upstairs and Rakim went too. You know he's worried someone will steal our baby." We both let out a laugh.

"I'll be the same when Mari delivers. Are you gonna marry him?" I chuckled.

"I don't know why?"

"Because mommy used to always say whoever you had kids by, you had to be married to. Shit, Mari wants to be my wife before she delivers. I'm surprised you don't feel the same."

"If I had a baby by Benji, then absolutely but Rakim is different and not in a bad way. He just learned how to be with one woman. Can you imagine tryna get him to be a married man?" He gave me a crazy look.

"I'm not saying he'll cheat. I'm just saying its gonna take longer." I shrugged and smiled when he showed me a baby picture of him holding me when I was young. Once my mom passed, we made sure to keep all photos and memorabilia.

"I didn't know you had this on the phone." I went through his photos.

"Mari wanted to see what I looked like as a kid. I screenshot and saved them." I kept scrolling and saw some of my mom too.

"Ok, you could've warned me." I handed him the phone back and he started cracking up. There were pictures of Mari dressed in lingerie and I noticed the play icon on some. I didn't wanna see the photos and damn sure not any videos.

"What you thought my fiancé wouldn't send me sexy pictures or videos? I'm sure that nigga has some of you."

"Whatever. You could've stopped me."

"Hi, mommy. Look who's here to see you." The nurse came in with my baby and I sat up quickly. She handed him to me and I just broke down crying.

"What's wrong? Did something happen to my nephew?" Mari barged in the room. She wasn't playing about coming in when the nurse brought him.

"Nothing. Come here sexy." Jose stood her in front of him.

"You wanna hold him?" I asked my brother. I'm sure Rakim already held him.

"He's too small."

"What about when our baby comes?" He shrugged her off and she took him from me. One by one, people started coming in. All their siblings, parents, our close friends and relatives as well. The room was packed and I had yet to see Rakim. Where the hell did he go?

Rakim

"Ok daddy. He's 6 lbs. 2 ounces and 18 inches long. We're gonna clean him up and take him back downstairs." The doctor said after checking him over.

When Jocelyn was delivering my ass had so many things going on in my head. I worried if my kid would come out ok, if she'd be ok after delivering and why wasn't she my wife already? I heard her say to one of her friends on the phone before that she wanted to be married before having kids.

It's been hard as hell being with one woman and seeing all these other ones out here, tryna fuck but I haven't cheated since she left me the first time. I think I'm too scared she won't come back the next time. Regardless; of my arrogant behavior she is a woman who won't let me walk over her.

Once the doctor told me my son was good, the nurse had me follow her to take him downstairs to Jocelyn. I told her to go ahead and left the hospital. It wasn't my intention to leave but there was something I needed to do. I made plans to do it after watching my brother kill Nika, but Jocelyn went into early labor, therefore; it had to wait.

I parked in front of my house, jumped out, grabbed the baby bag and hers and went to my car. I locked the door and turned to see this dumb bitch standing there. Her clothes appeared to be painted on and even though the pussy was good, I'd never touch her again. Her giving me a disease was most definitely an eye opener.

"What Ranisha?" I placed the bags in the car and closed the door.

"She gets Louis Vuitton bags and all I got was cash when you hit me off." I laughed.

"She can get whatever she wants because not only is she my girl, but she just had my son." Her mouth was on the floor.

"How do you know he's even yours?" She had her arms folded.

"Because I was the only nigga she fucked, unlike you."

"Rakim, I'm in love with you and I'm sorry."

"And I'm in love with her. She's gonna be my wife so I suggest you look elsewhere." I smiled at myself for calling her my future wife.

I noticed the tears rolling down her face. It's no secret she had feelings for me but I've never had any for her. I cared about her and didn't let anyone fuck with her but those days are gone.

"No Rakim. We're gonna be together. I'll stay quiet and be the side chick like before. Please don't leave me." She tried wrapping her arms around my neck. Just as I removed them, I saw Jose and two of his friends getting out a car.

"Yo! My sister just had your son and you're here with this bitch. Tha fuck type shit you on?" He took his shirt off and walked up on me. We never got the fight out from before.

"That's right. He's where he wanna be." Ranisha shouted.

"Bitch are you crazy?" I could see the three of them looking confused.

"Rakim why are you acting like that in front of her brother? The bitch don't fuck you like me."

"What did you say?" I walked up on her and she backed up.

"She don't..."

188

"Nah, you called her a bitch and what we do in the bedroom doesn't concern you. Get your ass off my property and don't ever come here again. If I see you ride down my motherfucking street, I'm gonna blow your got damns brains out. Do I make myself clear?"

"How she gonna speak and you have her by the throat with her eyes popping out." I heard someone say behind me. I dropped her and she hit the ground real hard.

"Stupid bitch."

"What's up? We fighting or what because I need to get to the hospital."

"It's whatever." Just as we were about to fight his friend stepped in the middle.

"Y'all need to chill."

"Nah, this nigga got a hand problem." Jose was as mad, as I.

"Ok fine. Y'all fight, then what? Huh? You're with his sister and he's with yours. So what y'all gonna hate each other forever? Mari, Jocelyn and the kids are the one who are gonna suffer. Is that what y'all want?"

"I don't give a fuck. All I know is he better treat my sister right and if you ever put hands on Mari again, I'm not gonna give a fuck about her being mad." He stormed off towards the car.

"I'm gonna ride with him." Tito said and I stood there waiting for this dumb bitch to get up.

"Rakim, how...?"

"I think it's in your best interest not to say another word." Tito told her and she pulled off.

I sat in my car and unlocked the other door for him to get in. Not that I wanted this nigga to ride with me but I ain't wanna leave him at my house either. He got in, asked if he could smoke a cigarette and rolled the window down.

The ride was quiet until my phone rang from Jocelyn asking where did I go? I mentioned picking the bags up and she seemed to feel relieved. I should've told her but I figured all the people would keep her occupied. I hung up and dude finally spoke.

"What's your beef with Jose?" At first, I didn't respond. It really wasn't a problem, I just wanted better for my sister.

"I don't like how my sister had to fight over him in the beginning and I feel like she deserves better."

"You don't think he feels the same about his sister." I looked over at him.

"Shit, we were all used to corny ass Benji. He was safe, corny, wasn't a cheater, always around and again, safe. We didn't have to worry about no bitches coming around to fight her or even him getting caught up on the streets while they were together. And I say we because even though you may not have seen us around a lot, we're still very close." I understood. You don't have to be around people 24/7 to consider them close.

"But look what happened when she dated a safe nigga. He cheated, got another bitch pregnant and supposedly cheated on her too. So I say good for her leaving him. Now someone else has to deal with his shit."

"Mari was hurt by a dude she felt was her everything. However; he obviously didn't feel the same because he cheated and told people she's the reason he did it."

"Huh?"

"Mari wasn't putting out like most women and he used it as an excuse to dip out. She left him alone and he started dogging her out real bad. One of the chicks even taped them having sex and him calling her names. She didn't wanna tell us so when I went to visit a chick I was fucking at her school, I overheard him and beat the fuck outta him. Ever since, I've been very protective of her and it may not be right in other people's eyes but it is, what it is." We pulled up at the hospital.

"I understand but Jose ain't in the street like he used to be. He's never been a man to cheat on his woman and I know that first hand." I gave him a look because all men cheat at least once.

"I kid you not. Shit, back in the day I tried to get him to cheat on that crazy bitch Dutchess and he refused. The way he loved Dutchess is nothing like the way he loves Mari though."

"What you mean?"

"He was with his ex for two years and never thought to put a ring on her finger. Your sister got him to do it in less than a year. Whatever your sister is doing to him, minus the sex, has him deep in love." We opened the car doors and stepped out.

192

"Look Rakim. I get you wanting to protect your sister and so does he. As her man, he won't allow anything to happen to her. Then, she has y'all and now us. Her, Jocelyn and everyone else marrying or dating within the two families will always have people watching their backs. It's called loyalty and trust. Y'all are all you got and we're the same." The doors opened and we went to the elevators.

"If you and Mari plan on being with them, I suggest you and Jose learn to get along or expect a lotta arguments and lonely nights. If you haven't noticed those two women are all about family and getting together. Trust it's going to be a bunch of events you're at, at the same time."

"I got it and thanks for the talk. I never really looked at it in any other way."

"He has but he also sees how much his sister loves you and backed off. You have to do the same or Jocelyn will leave you." He patted my shoulder and walked in the room before me. *Would she really leave me?*

****

"Where you been nigga? How you leaving when she had your baby?" Jose pulled her close to him.

"Be quiet Mari."

"No because…" He covered her mouth and everyone else got quiet. Jocelyn used her hands to cover hers.

"Rakim." She had tears coming down her face.

"I made plans to do this at home before you delivered but my son couldn't wait, so it's no time like the present." She nodded and let the tears continue to fall.

"I don't really know what to say. I'm just gonna go off the top of my head." She tried to wipe her tears but they continued falling.

"When I did you wrong and you left me, I thought it was the end of the world. I couldn't eat, sleep or even focus because you weren't in my life. That's when I knew you were perfect for me. The way you demanded respect and walked away no matter how much you loved me, showed how strong of a woman you truly are and I couldn't allow anyone to take you away from me. Jocelyn Alvarado, you are the air I breathe and I wanna know if you'll be my wife?" She nodded her head, kissed and hugged me tight.

I moved back and slid the ring on her finger. My mom actually helped me pick it out for her and I'm glad she did because I didn't know how to pick one. Unfortunately, the price was fucking ridiculous but she's more than worth it.

"Who knew your ignorant ass could be sentimental?" Mari pushed me on my arm, then hugged me.

"You guys get a different version but he's always that way with me." Jocelyn held her hand out to stare at the ring. Her cousin and the other women were gawking over it. She's right. I could never get upset with her for some reason.

"Jose, I apologize for the shit with my sister and you. I thought you were bad for her and it wasn't until someone spoke some real shit and made me realize, you're the best man for her. You protect her even against family and I admire that because most niggas don't even get in the middle. She loves you and I don't want no beef because then I have to deal with my future wife's attitude. I don't ever wanna go through the silent treatment with her again in any way."

195

"As long as you don't put your hands on either of them, I'm good. Sister or not, she's my woman and I will have her back at all costs. And I apologize for not telling you we were a couple. I was working for you but she made me promise to give her time and she knows how to keep me quiet that's for sure."

"Yuk!" Jocelyn shouted making everyone laugh.

"Excuse me! Excuse me! God daddy coming through." George bombarded his way through everyone.

"What are you doing?" I asked when he pulled a bunch of clothes out a bag.

"Ugh, I need to see which outfit he's going to where at his Christening. You do know he has to be in either Gucci or Versace. Ain't no slouching over here. Now let me see." He placed the clothes against lil Rakim's body as my mom held him. Everyone was laughing and Levi was shaking his head. I have to say whether I wanted a gay brother or not, George is a perfect addition to our family.

"I'm so glad you and Jose made up." Jocelyn patted the seat next to her. Everyone left an hour ago because visiting hours were over. She had the nurse help as she cleaned up again and change the sheets.

"Yea well, I knew you'd hold out on this good ass pussy and I can't have that. Especially; when you do those tricks and shit." She tossed her head back laughing.

"Whatever. Are you sure about getting married?" She put her hand out again to look at the ring. I can't even count how many times she did it.

"Positive. There's no other woman deserving of me, then you."

"What happened at the house?" She stared at me. I knew her brother would fill her in, which is why Mari snapped when I arrived. I told her what happened and she was ready to fight.

"You're a mother now ma. No more fighting. Plus, I don't think she'll return."

"She better not or I'm gonna take her out myself since you didn't."

"Baby, if she needs to die she will but right now her feelings are hurt because I didn't choose her."

"Yea, yea. Gimme a kiss." She poked her lips out and I leaned in to kiss her. My son started squirming on my chest.

"Uh oh. Don't look like you'll be allowed to touch me in front of him."

"Whatever." I kissed her again and he did the same." She tends to think he's gonna be a momma's boy but he better not.

Efrain

"Ok Efrain. I think that's enough for the day." Geri stood and went to the desk.

"How much longer do I have to come here?" She sat down and I stood in front of her desk. I never touched or kissed her here because now that we're a couple, I didn't wanna make her feel uncomfortable at work or have a colleague or someone walk in.

"Efrain you definitely made progress and the fact you can speak on the situation without becoming aggressive is great."

"Does that mean I don't have to return?"

"It's always good to attend therapy but it's really up to you."

"I don't want to but you're the doctor. You tell me?"

"Ok. Do you feel like these sessions are helping you outside of the office? I mean do you find yourself coping in the workplace, when negative situations arise, and can you honestly say you use the relaxing mechanism we went over?"

"Yea, I do all that. At work no one bothers me because of who my family is and at home, I have flashbacks once in a while, but not like before."

"Let's do this. We'll have a session once a week now and if you need more, we can." I agreed because this four times a week shit was becoming too much. Hell, I didn't wanna come at all but I knew discussing it in front of my family doesn't make it all go away.

"Fine. I'll see you later."

"Ok." She tried to kiss me but I backed away.

"Is something wrong?"

"Geri, I thought we discussed not doing that because we didn't want anyone coming in." She pushed the chair out, stood, walked to the door, locked it and came to where I was.

"Lucky for us, its Saturday and no one is here. Therefore; we can do whatever." She unbuttoned her shirt, tossed it on the floor and once her bra let her tities spill out, my dick grew.

"Damn." She lifted one of her breasts up and licked it with her tongue.

"Don't you want me Efrain?" I took my shirt off.

"That's one question you never have to ask." Our mouths met and the way our tongues greeted one another had us both tryna rip each other's clothes off. This will be the first time we had sex. I can't even tell you why we waited but I'm glad we did because right now I'm ready to do whatever.

"Are you ok with this Efrain?" I knew she was asking me because the truth is, I haven't been with anyone since the shit happened.

"I'm fine. Got damn." She went down and sucked the hell outta my dick.

"How does it feel baby?" She now had my balls in her mouth as her fingers were juggling under.

"Real good. I'm about to… Shit." I came so hard, I held on to the desk to keep from falling. Playing with yourself and having someone actually do it, has two different feelings that's for sure. I felt her tongue tracing up my body and my man began to grow slowly.

"It's been a while Geri but let me see if I still got it." I led her to the couch, laid her down and spread her legs. She was a thick woman so of course her pussy was fat but the way her juices slid out had me ready to fuck.

I didn't want her to think I changed my mind and dove in. Her scent was a strawberry smell and the way she fucked my face, let me know she was enjoying it. Once my two fingers entered, her body shook and I tasted her nectar.

"Shit Efrain. Let me get a minute." She attempted to push me away. I moved her hands, gripped her ass and dug my face in between her legs again. I had her screaming, gripping the couch and creaming more than I ever seen. I mean she definitely had the wet, wet.

"You ready?" She nodded her head yes and grabbed me in for a kiss.

"Hold on Efrain. It's been a while for me too." I gave her two seconds and plunged inside.

It's been a long time since I've been inside a woman, how could she expect me to wait. The second I got all the way in because she was super tight, I had to stop a few times to keep from cumming.

"You feel so fucking good Geri." Her juices were seeping out as I maneuvered in and out. I stood, lifted her legs and watched myself take her to ecstasy. I thought it would be hard and memories would surface but nope. It was all about us and the feeling was amazing.

"I need to see this ass from the back." She smiled, turned around and let me drill as far as I wanted.

"Fuck Efrain. I'm about to cum again. Keep going. Don't stop. Yesssss." I saw her juices rush out. A few minutes later, I pulled out and squirted all over her ass and smacked it. I wasn't ready for no kids. I can see my nephews and whatever Mari has if I wanna be around them.

"Shit." She was lying on the couch breathing heavy.

"I hope you were satisfied." She turned to look at me and sat on her knees to straddle me. I felt her lower half grinding on me.

"You did more than satisfy me Efrain. I definitely want more." She started sucking on my neck and got me back up.

"Go slow." I told her when she navigated down my shaft with her banging ass pussy.

"I'll do whatever you want baby." She began riding me and I couldn't help but grab her waist and slam her down on it. I wanted her to feel me deep in her stomach and know that no one will fuck her this good. We're not in love by any means but I don't plan on sleeping with anyone else either.

I saw my brother Rakim stress himself out when he got caught cheating, or should I say sleeping with Ranisha because he wasn't claiming Jocelyn yet. I have enough problems and don't need anymore. A woman like Geri has too much going for herself and don't need a man. If I cheat, she's the type not to give second chances and right now, I need all the pussy I can get to make up for years without it.

"You staying the night?" She asked when I pulled up at her house. We spent the entire day exploring one another in her office.

"Is that what you want?" I figured she wanted to shower and be alone but I guess not. We both cleaned up before we left but it's nothing like taking a shower to feel better.

"Ugh yea. What if I require this is the morning?" She reached over and grabbed my dick.

"Ride with me to my house to grab some clothes and we can grab something to eat on the way back." She put her seatbelt back on.

"Whatever you say daddy." She kissed my cheek. I smiled and thought about all the shit we're about to do at her house.

****

"I'll have the steak and shrimp well done with the baked potato." Geri ordered her food and handed the waitress back the menu. We were originally going to grab something in a drive thru but decided to go sit in a diner.

"How's the baby?" She referred to my nephew.

"Good. It's been two weeks since she delivered and Rakim said my mom, George and Mari been acting like stalkers. They come over everyday after work and my mom is there most of the day to help her out, when Rakim isn't home."

"That's good. Your family is very tight and it's good to see all of them coming together."

205

"Yea, but we're not perfect as you can tell."

"No family is regardless; of what they portray on the outside. Take yours for example. Had I not met you, I would've assumed there wasn't one issue within your household."

"Why is that?" I sipped the beer and someone caught my eye but it couldn't be.

"Your family is rich, everyone has their own place, in a relationship and most of you are always around one another. I'm telling you on the outside looking in, you can't tell."

"Let me talk to you real quick." I looked up and saw the nightmare that wouldn't go away standing there. Geri noticed the look on my face and instantly picked her phone up. She's probably contacting Rakim. He told her if we're ever out and any of these assholes approached me, for her to call or text. He knew I wouldn't because I'd be ready to kill them, like I am now.

"I'm good Bobby."

"Bobby?" I heard Geri whisper and look at him. I'm sure she figured out this is the same person I spoke of in therapy.

"I wasn't asking you." My leg began shaking under the table.

"I'm here on a date with my woman. Whatever you have to say can wait until we meet another time and trust me when I say, we will." I gave him a smirk.

"I said..." I jumped out my seat.

"And I said, not today."

"Efrain this is not the place for it. Let's go." She went to grab my hand and he slapped it away.

"Nigga are you fucking crazy? Don't put your hands on my woman."

"Efrain please." I grabbed her hand and walked out the diner tryna calm myself down.

"HEY! YOU KNOW YOU"RE FUCKING WITH A GAY NIGGA RIGHT?" I froze and noticed Geri getting ready to cry.

"What the fuck you say?"

"YOU BETTER HOPE THE NIGGA DON'T HAVE AIDS. YOU KNOW WHAT THEY SAY ABOUT GAY MEN!" That was it. I couldn't take anymore. I knew AIDS didn't run through my body because I took a test twice a year just to make sure.

CLICK! I had the gun against his temple.

"Keep talking shit nigga and I'm gonna blow your head off in front of this diner." His hands went up.

"Oh now you scared? What happened to the tough guy in the diner popping all that shit? Where he go?" I heard a car screech and smiled. I didn't have to turn around to figure out who it was. We were local and if she did indeed call Rakim, I knew he sent whoever was close.

"You're about to get what's coming to you." I put the gun in my waist and waited for Rakim's dudes to come take him away. He was yelling and trying his hardest to get away.

"Let's go." I took Geri's hand in mine and went to my car. It's obvious we won't be eating here. I drove back to her house, waited for her to open the door and went straight in the bathroom.

"You ok?"

"Yup." She stepped in the shower with me and stared.

"I'm proud of you Efrain." I gave her the side eye.

"I am. You could've killed him but you didn't. It's not to say you won't but you were able to keep it together and for that you deserve an award. Let me be the one to give it to you." When she fell to her knees to please me, I was tryna think of ways to get in trouble and get out of it, just to get these kinds of rewards. Hell yea, I'm keeping her around.

Talia

"I don't know Dutchess. From what I hear, Jose is getting better and he's looking for you." This crazy bitch wants to see him for some reason.

After she had him purposely shot, she's been on the run. Supposedly they had her in some witness protection program but she's actually with her sister.

When Jose knocked me out some woman helped me up in just enough time to see him reaching for Mari. Dutchess yelled out he had a gun and Jose went down. I ran over to see if he were ok as his girl beat the crap outta her. I don't think she realized I was standing there because she probably would've been ready to fight me. I still have nightmares witnessing the blood pouring out his body.

I did get in my feelings when he called out for her. However; if I didn't learn shit from the Ethan situation, I learned from this one. Jose was madly in love with Mari and nothing I or Dutchess could do or say would change it. This is one defeat I have to take like a champ. Ain't no getting in between but it doesn't hurt to try.

See, it was easy for me to get in the middle of her and Ethan because the nigga wasn't shit. He had been screwing all the women around town and probably in other places, yet I'm the only one he stayed around the longest. I know that because I pushed them away the same way I did Mari.

It's been plenty of nights he came through confessing his love for her but somehow ended up fucking me all night. One time he called me her name and that was it.

I blacked out on him and asked how could he treat me that way. Eventually, he apologized and began dogging Mari out. He called her all types of bitches, saying she was a virgin and a bunch of other stuff. I guess it was to save face. Little did he know it was too late. I recorded him saying those things and us having sex. When he went to sleep, I got her number out his phone and sent it to her. She was devastated to say the least because she shut down from what I hear.

Long story short, her brother Rakim came up and Ethan was talking shit about her to some other guys. I think it was to impress them but her brother wasn't tryna hear it and almost killed him. Meanwhile, my ass was a tad bit nervous because I had been harassing the fuck outta her. Making untrue posts about her on FB, and other dumb shit. That's why when she saw me at the restaurant with Jose and Jocelyn she asked him to keep it moving. Who knew there was another crazy brother sitting with her.

"Look, his sister recently had the baby and I know the bitch he's with has been there a lot. I need you to follow her to the house and let me know. It will give me time to go see him." I had to look at my phone.

"Are you crazy? He will kill you." She thought my response was hilarious.

"He and I have history. Kill me? Not at all. Fuck me? Absolutely. He never could deny me."

"Dutchess."

"JUST DO IT!" She shouted and hung up. The only reason I even entertained doing it is because she's a cop and I definitely don't wanna be shot like Jose.

I looked at the time and it was six, which means Mari is already off or about to get off. I didn't have a lotta time, hopped in my car and raced over to the bank. Crazy as it may seem the bitch had just walked out the building. I can't front. Even with the big belly she was still gorgeous. I can see why Jose is with her if it's based off looks. Her style of dress is decent too.

I watched as she sat in her expensive ass car and became jealous. I don't know if he purchased it or not but so what. She had my man, and I want him back. Dutchess can be mad all she wants but I'm getting ready to run this ho off the road.

I waited for her to back up and as I was getting ready to go behind her, my car door opened and my body was yanked on the ground. I couldn't speak because someone had their foot on my neck.

"I can crush your fucking throat and it wouldn't be a thing you could do." I heard his voice but the sun was in my eyes so I couldn't see him. He pressed harder on my neck and it felt like my life started slipping away. I couldn't breathe and my eyes were bulging.

"I'm gonna take my foot off your neck and you're gonna tell me why the hell you watching my fiancé." He did it and I gasped for air as he lifted me up by my shirt. The facial expression he wore let me know he's gonna kill me.

"Dutchess sent me." I finally got out. He dropped me and searched the parking lot.

"She's not here."

"You good?" I looked and another fine man came to where we were with a female.

"Talia said…"

"Talia?" The woman questioned.

"Yea." The minute he said it, the chick started banging my head into the side of the car. The punches hurt real bad and it took both of them a minute to get her off me.

"That's for Mari and all the dumb shit you were doing to her."

WHAP! She smacked fire from me. I went to grab her hair and the dude pushed me so hard I fell back and hit my head on the concrete.

"Let me have Rakim let his people come get her." Jose nodded and I tried to run but it was no use. He had the back of my shirt.

Ten minutes later a black van pulled up and two guys stepped out. They asked him what he wanted to do with me and he told them, he didn't care as long as I wasn't breathing in the next half hour. I began screaming, crying and begging them not to do it. Unfortunately, it all fell on deaf ears as my body was thrown in the back.

There weren't any seats and as they drove, my body rolled all over. When it stopped, I heard the two guys laughing. Once the door opened and I realized we were at a lake, I knew my fate. I said my prayers silently as they drug me to the water. I thought they'd toss me in but nope. One pointed a gun at me, while the other poured gasoline over my body.

"What... what are you doing?"

"First, I'm gonna shoot you in the stomach and then set you on fire. That way you can feel the effects of both." He gave me a fake smile and two seconds later I felt an excruciating pain in my stomach. Both of them laughed as he lit me on fire. I felt everything and it seemed like it took forever for me to die. I smelled my flesh burning and vomited before succumbing to my death. I should've never listened to Dutchess but I'm sure she'll be joining me soon.

Mari

"Mmmm baby, I have to go." I tried to pull myself away from Jose.

Today I was having lunch with my mom, Genesis and Jocelyn to go over things for my wedding. Heck yea, I'm trying to get it done before I have the baby. Yet, here he is lying in the bed naked with only a sheet covering him. The tattoos on his upper body were showing and the way he stared at me always and I mean always, turned me on.

This man had such an effect on me, I couldn't walk away even if I wanted to. So here I am fresh out the shower, dropping my towel and going towards the bed after I promised myself I'd be strong. But with a man like mine, ain't no way. Even at six and a half months with a belly in the way, I'm still able to please him.

I let our tongues play around for a few minutes before trailing kisses down his neck. I took my time spelling my name on his chest with my tongue. It sounds crazy but if you're sexy with it he'll love it.

I continued down to his stomach and let my tongue dip in and out his belly button, then moved to the inside of his legs and kissed the tip. I opened my mouth to swallow him, looked up to wink and went to work on that dick.

"Yea ma. Do that shit Mari." One hand gripped the sheet as the other had my hair. I let my tongue do all types of tricks and as he grew, I juggled his balls with my fingers and sucked under where it's very sensitive but not his ass. When he started to twitch I went back to sucking. When I felt his dick touching my throat and I started humming. I wanted to see if what chicks say really worked and I'll be damned.

"Yoooooo!!!! Fuckkkkkk!!!!" He legs shook and he had my hair in a death grip. I don't think I've even witnessed him release this hard. I tried to kiss him afterwards and he pushed me away and told me to hold on. Yea, a bitch had to pat herself on the back.

I kissed his lips, went in the bathroom to shower again. The minute I leaned over to shut it on, I felt him behind me. Instead of turning around I walked over to the toilet, put the lid down, grabbed the back of the tank and lifted my leg. We're not about to make love this morning. He's getting ready to fuck the shit outta me because he's not the type to be outdone in the bedroom.

"You already know what time it is, don't you?" His fingers slid up and down my middle and then inside.

"Sssss. Yes baby. Give it to me." He had me fuck his fingers first and without warning, rammed himself inside.

"You think you're the shit for sucking my soul out huh?" He was sucking on my neck as he pounded harder.

"Yup and thanks for telling me I am." He chuckled and went even harder.

"Jose baby." He moved me off the toilet and now had me facing the wall, leg spread open and one in the crook of his arm.

"You're gonna make me cummmmmmmmm....." I couldn't hold it and let go. I tried to take a break but nope.

"Ain't no breaks Mari." He swung me around and for a quick second both of us stared into each other's eyes.

"You really are the love of my life Mari."

"And you're my soulmate baby." He crashed his lips on mine and the two of us went at it like rabbits in the bathroom and took it to the bedroom. Being pregnant and horny all the time sure has its perks when it comes to a man with a hefty sexual appetite.

"I can't wait to make you my wife."

"And I can't wait to be an Alvarado." He smiled, kissed the top of my forehead and seconds later I was knocked out.

****

"Demaris Davis are you kidding me?" I heard my mothers voice but it's no way she's at Jose's house. She's never been here and I damn sure didn't invite her.

I rolled over and Jose was missing but her, Jocelyn and Genesis were standing there staring at me. I threw the covers over my head and laughed at how aggravated they looked. My mom pulled the covers back and lucky I was on my side because they would've saw a lot more than they bargained for.

"How are we supposed to be setting up for your wedding next month and you laid up?"

"Ma, Jose.-"

"Don't blame him. He's been by the house talking to your father for about an hour now."

"What? What time is it?"

"Three o' clock." I got out the shower this morning around 10:30 so I could make the 11:30 lunch. I don't even know what time he and I finished and now she's telling me it's after 3. Then, my fiancé bounced without waking me up and here they are grilling the shit outta me.

"Ok. It's only going to take me a few minutes to get ready."

"Yea well hurry up. I'm hungry." Genesis said and I laughed. She wasn't far along in her pregnancy yet but Dash said she's eating like crazy.

"Ok. Do y'all mind tho?" I sat up with the cover over my chest.

"Just get in the shower." Jocelyn barked and left with Genesis. My mom sat down on the chair Jose had in here he played that stupid game on.

"I'm so proud of you Mari." I grabbed my robe off the end of the bed and put it on. She's my mother so I don't care if she sees me.

"You met a man who worships the ground you walk on, stood up to your brother, you're having my next grand baby and getting married. You have no idea how happy your father and I are."

"Thanks, but…"

"Honey we thought with the way your brothers act you'd end up with a guy you really didn't love and be bored for the rest of your life." I laughed.

"But Jose. Chile, not only is he handsome."

"I'm telling daddy." She and I both shared a laugh. She stood and came over to me.

"He brings out the best in you Mari and whether Rakim says it or not, he knows it too."

"You think I'll keep him happy? What if he falls out of love or sees one of those nasty heffas at a club and.-"

"Don't speak on something that won't happen. If he wanted to cheat he would've done it already and from what

Dash says, he's too scared you'll leave him if he even looks at another woman."

"I love him so much mommy. He's like the air I breathe and I get excited everyday waking up knowing he's going to be right next to me."

"I know and so does he." She turned me around and he was leaning on the door smiling.

"I'm not going anywhere Mari, ever. So stop thinking about the what if's." He came towards me and my mom walked out closing the door behind her.

"It's not a woman out here who can make me cheat on you." I put my hand over his as he held my face.

"I know my ex makes you have some doubt but I'm telling you she won't ever get me again." He pecked my lips, opened my robe and kneeled down in front of me.

"I can't wait to meet you." His lips were cold on my belly and felt good at the same time. He rubbed my stomach a few times and stood.

"You do know they're gonna talk shit, right?" He led me in the bathroom and started the shower.

"Why didn't you wake me up?"

"You looked peaceful."

"But you knew I had to go." He turned and removed the robe.

"All you have to do is stand there and my dick gets hard." I looked down and sure enough he was sticking straight up.

"Well since I know how to make you cum in more ways than one, let me help you out real quick." He closed the bathroom door, locked it and stripped.

"This dick is fucking perfect." I stroked him and he had me sit on the bench in his shower. At times like this, it sure came in handy. I handled my man, let him wash me up and got out to get dressed. He tried to give me some, but I knew I'd be ready to sleep so I passed but he promised to do me later.

"Can we go now?" My mom had lil Rakim in her arms, as Genesis and Jocelyn were watching television and talking.

"I'm ready."

"Next time don't ask us to come out to eat. Just show up and we'll go from there."

"Don't come for my fiancé." He held me from behind and placed a soft kiss on my neck.

"I won't be here when you return and don't wait up." I turned to look at him.

"Don't ask questions." I nodded and he walked me to his truck. He wanted me driving it because my car was too low.

"Be careful babe. You know she's probably got people watching." I knew he was going after Dutchess because we spoke about it last night. Supposedly, she had been staying with her sister and contacting Talia. I guess she didn't know the type of brothers I had.

Jose had Talia's phone tapped, which is how he found out she would be around. We had no idea she'd show up at our job but it didn't surprise us. When security called upstairs and said a woman pulled into the parking lot after business hours, all of us looked outside. We weren't sure it was her though.

Jose didn't want me to go out first but when he realized it was her, he knew she didn't have a gun. I assumed she'd get out and approach me, however; she stayed and waited for me to get in my car. Jose snatched her ass out and I can't even tell you what happened afterwards.

As far as Dutchess, Levi traced the call to a house in Philadelphia. Now being a cop, detective or whatever she is on the force, one would think her stupid ass would block the number or hang up before two minutes. Not Dutchess. She thought her ass was invincible and fucked up. Now my man and his boys were on their way to get her and I couldn't wait for him to kill her. She was a pain in the ass and needed to die. Jose, couldn't wait because we all know she's the one who had him shot.

"Always. I love you ma. Text me when you get home later."

"I'm gonna stay with my parents or Jocelyn."

"Why?"

"I'm going to worry myself to death if I don't have company and I'll text and call you all night." He started laughing and told me I can call whenever I feel like it. He'd answer even if he had a knife to her throat.

"Ok, already." Jocelyn pulled up on the side of us.

"Go ahead Mari before I kick my sister's ass."

"I love you Jose." He shut the door and leaned in to kiss me.

"I love you too and I'll make sure to be extra safe to make it home to you and my baby. Plus, ain't no man ever walking down that aisle with you but me." He patted the top of the truck and I pulled off. I said a prayer asking God to keep him safe.

"It's about time. Got me starving." George fanned himself. He met us here because Dash had him come in for a few hours to catch up on whatever Maxine didn't do. Evidently, she's been slacking on her position for a while; per Genesis.

"You can blame your fake ass best friend who can't seem to stay out the bedroom." He sucked his teeth as we all took a seat.

"Now you two hush. Had Dashier not been busy this morning, Rakim out with Efrain and Levi watching Kingston, I'm sure y'all would be doing the same thing."

"I know I would." George said without hesitation.

"Not going to give y'all too much because what me and my man do is private but when Levi and I do our thing; neither one of us leaving the house."

"George what did I tell you about that?"

"I'm sorry ma but Jocelyn brought it up." My mouth dropped and he flipped me the bird. She always told us on the few breakfast and lunch dates we've gone on, that bedroom stories are off limits in front of her.

"Now pass me my God baby. He's finished eating off that big ass titty. You really should pump more to get the milk out. They're too big for your body."

"Really!" Mari shouted.

"I'm just saying. Jocelyn is small and her tities are huge. It looks funny." He shrugged his shoulders and Ms. Davis shook her head. Genesis didn't know what to say where I'm use to his ignorance now.

"You know if Levi weren't with you he'd be all over these." I lifted my son up to burp him and made sure the cover was over my breasts.

I know there's a huge controversy over breastfeeding in public and that's fine. I have no problem feeding my son wherever, whenever, however; strangers do not need to see my breasts. And using a cover is not because I'm ashamed. My man will have a fit if anyone sees a part of my body that's only for him.

"Girl if ma wasn't here, I promise I'd say something else." He stood and took lil Rakim from me. I definitely appreciated him and everyone else in my life right now. They were truly a blessing helping me with the baby.

"Ok so let's focus on me now. This is what I want for the wedding." Mari spoke and the event planner took a ton of notes. Mari had to call and ask her to come back because she assumed the brunch was cancelled and went home.

"What type of food for the reception?" The lady asked and Mari looked at me.

"Jocelyn what kind of food does he like besides the normal?" I gave her a list of Hispanic foods and told her my aunt has a restaurant in Newark. She's met some of my family but not all of them. They were all at the hospital but because she couldn't come they never got the chance to be introduced.

"He did tell me about her. Do you think she'll be able to make some trays?"

"I'll call but I'm sure she'll have no issues making it."

"Yeaaaaa! I want to make sure he knows I'm including him too."

"He knows weirdo." I picked my fork up to eat my salad and instantly caught an attitude. How is this bitch even walking the streets?

"Where's Talia?" Ranisha stopped at the table with her hand on her hips. No one answered so she asked again. This time directing the question to Mari.

"Talia is wherever she is so I suggest you move on."

"Nah she's with your man. Do me a favor and tell her after she sends him home, to call me." We all knew Talia was dead but mentioning her name bothered Mari. I guess it would being she tried to bring up the fact they were having sex.

"Ranisha, do we have a problem?" It was at that moment she recognized me.

"You would be with this bitch."

"Bitch?" I questioned and tossed my napkin on the table.

"Hold up. Take my Godson." He passed lil Rakim to Genesis and stood.

"I got this George." He moved to where Ranisha stood.

"I know you do but I also know your fiancé…" He grabbed my hand and held it up for her to see. Her eyes got watery.

"Your fiancé Rakim doesn't want his woman fighting anymore. You're a mother and should conduct yourself in such a way. Therefore; since this manly looking woman is here talking shit, it's only right I handle it."

"George you can't fight a woman." Mari stood and Ranisha sucked her teeth. She was real mad staring at her belly.

"Oh you thought Jose would've gotten Talia pregnant?" She laughed at her.

"Honey she may have had him first but once taste of me and he never looked back. So before you come in here barking orders about my man, think about why the one you desperately seek doesn't want you."

"Fuck y'all." You heard glasses shatter and people gasp as her body hit the table from George mushing her.

"I may be a man sweetie but one thing you won't do in front of me is disrespect any of my sisters or mother." He lifted her by the shirt.

"I will beat your ass in this restaurant and my gay ass won't do a day in jail."

"GET OFF ME!"

"Now you tough." He moved closer to her ear.

"You better watch your back because once my man, Rakim, Dash and Jose hear how you came in here talking shit. I can guarantee you'll be joining your friend. Now beat it bitch." He pushed her away and this time she hit the ground.

"Call the cops please." She screamed out.

"Ma'am you have to go." The manager told her.

"But..."

"But I saw you step into my boss's place of business to harass his sister, fiancé and guests. Do you really expect me to call the police on them?" She got up and fixed her clothes.

"Oh but you better believe he saw everything." He turned the phone to us and Rakim was on FaceTime. He handed it to me.

"Y'all good?"

"Yea. She came questioning Mari about Talia, and called me a bitch. You know the normal."

"How's my son and mom?" I turned the phone and she was having a conversation with everyone at our table like nothing happened.

"Aight. Have fun and I'll see you later."

"Babe, I didn't know you owned a restaurant." He had a grin on his face.

"When you say I do; you'll know a lotta stuff. Until then, it's under wraps." He hung up and I gave the phone back to the manager.

"Do you need anything?" He asked and we told him no. I sat down smiling because at least I knew he did something with his money. I'm hoping he stops this street life shit and goes legal anyway. I won't give him an ultimatum because I feel if he wants to stop, he will. At least, I know he has something to fall back on.

Jose

"It's been a long time coming bro." Tito passed me the blunt and continued driving.

As you know we were on our way to Philadelphia. Dutchess definitely hid herself well and it's only because no one knew where her sister was. I thought she still resided in Jersey but when the guys went to the house, the person living there told them they've been in the place for the last five years. Whatever the case, she's been found and I dare her to try and save Dutchess. That bitch don't deserve to breathe any longer.

The best part about this operation is having Mari in my life because her brothers were definitely connected in many ways. Dash, hooked me up with Raphael and even though it was awkward because my sister dated his brother, he still helped. His crooked ass had law enforcement friends everywhere and for this mission, I needed them to stay away.

Levi is the one who found Dutchess and Rakim, had another team of dudes following behind the two trucks already with me. He claims it's to make up for treating Mari like his kid and not an adult. I get it but he went overboard. Shit, if I had no idea they were related I'd assume they were fucking.

"I can't even say she don't deserve this. Not only did she shoot me, she's still attempting to come for Mari and for what? My stroke game is definitely the shit but she bugging."

"Yo! Don't nobody wanna hear that shit." Raul barked and snatched the blunt out my hand from the back seat.

"Shut yo ass up. All the bitches you say be strung out on your ass."

"They do." Tito and I looked in the back seat and busted out laughing. How the hell is what I said any different?

"Hey ma." I answered for Mari as we got off the New Jersey Turnpike and went into Philadelphia.

"I miss you already." I smiled and put my head down so they didn't catch me blushing.

"I miss you too. You good?"

"Yea. But Ranisha approached me asking about Talia. Jocelyn almost beat her up but George stepped in and then the manager called Rakim. Baby it was a mess but I called to tell you, your aunt is catering a few dishes for the wedding."

"Make sure you have her make Empanadas."

"I did babe. I know they're your favorite."

"Nah, you're my favorite." I heard both of them suck their teeth.

"You're my favorite too and the only man who can make me cum off his voice. Babe can we have phone sex real quick?"

"Absolutely not and if you do, I promise to hang up. You'll just have to be mad." She hated for me to hang the phone up. I didn't do it a lot but she played too much and I had to a few times.

"Ok fine. You want me to send you a video?"

"I'm coming home tonight so whatever you want, I'll be there to give it to you."

"Bye Mari. We're at the spot." Raul yelled from the back and I looked up to see he wasn't lying.

"I'll hit you when I'm finished." We each put black gloves on and wore our baseball caps real low.

"Be safe Jose and don't even think about touching her inappropriately." I laughed and disconnected the call. We

237

parked a street over and I hit Raphael up. He assured me

everyone was on the same page, which is why I walked around

the corner with Tito and knocked on the door.

"I got it Marie. I'm waiting for the pizza guy." I had a

grin on my face when the bitch opened the door. She attempted

to close it but I bombarded my way in and backed her into a

wall.

"Is it the food?" Her sister came running in with money.

"What up Marie?" She froze and looked at me and Tito.

Tears began to roll down her face. I heard the door shut and

looked to see Raul and a few other guys. They went to each

room, checking to make sure no one else was here.

"Jose, I'm sorry." Dutchess tried pleading her case but

it was too late for regrets.

"Dutchess when you left years ago, did I not say we

were over and never to look for me again?" I stared at her body

shaking.

"Yes." I heard the fear in her voice.

"Not only did you ignore me, but tried to fight my girl,

who I must say beat the shit outta you and then, had me shot because I didn't want you. Last but not least, you wanted Talia to follow my girl so you could come to my house in hopes to rekindle a flame that's since been burnt out."

"Dutchess what did you do?" Now most would assume her sister may have been clueless but don't let her fake innocence fool you. The two of them are sisters as well as best friends. They told each other everything. I nodded and Tito put a bullet in between Marie's eyes.

"Was that necessary?"

"I could ask you the same question with all the extra bullshit you've been doing. However; I wanted you to know your entire family was wiped out because you couldn't stay away." I held her hand in mine and led her in the living room.

"This is what's gonna happen." I pointed to the couch for her to sit.

"You're gonna call the captain of your department and tell him you can't take it anymore and need to be with your parents. Afterwards…"

"I don't wanna die Jose. Can I apologize and…" I ignored her stupid ass.

"Afterwards, you're gonna go in the bathroom and sit in the tub Raul made for you."

"Please." She cried and a long time ago it may have gotten to me but not this time.

"If you would've left my woman alone we wouldn't be here. You're the same Dutchess from back then. When you can't get your way, you go and do drastic shit and get innocent people involved." I pointed at her sister dead on the floor.

"Then, try and cry your way outta shit. Not this time. Make the call." She had her head down and didn't move.

"You have ten seconds to get him on the phone or Raul and Tito are going to have fun with you." She lifted her head. They weren't going to rape her or anything like that. They loved to torture the fuck outta people and she's been around long enough to know how they get down. She snatched the phone out my hand and dialed a number.

CLICK! I don't give a fuck that you're gonna die. If you scream out anything, I promise to kill Marie's three-year-old son, who's at his father's house." Her mouth fell open.

240

Marie and her sons' father weren't together and shared custody. She was as crazy as Dutchess and he refused to be with her.

"I know everything so let me see if you're really that selfish." She wiped her face, dialed the number and did what I said.

Lucky for us, he wasn't at his desk, which means we had a little more time. I made her leave a voicemail, and handed the phone to Tito. I grabbed her ankles and slid her off the couch and her hit the ground hard as hell. I continued dragging her up the steps and could care less about the screaming and crying. I stopped in the bathroom, lifted her up and dropped her in the scolding hot water. She attempted to get out until I put my gun to her head.

"Watch out." Raul came in and poured the pot of hot water on her. He started boiling it as soon as he walked in the house. She was so busy tryna plead her case she never paid attention. Her skin was literally turning red and peeling that quick.

"It smells like gasoline. Jose please let me out." Tito handed me the matches.

"This is for almost making my girl lose my baby." I set the book of matches on fire and dropped it in the tub. All of us jumped back and watched her burn. The smell of her flesh invaded our nostrils and the scene was pretty horrific.

"We gotta go." One of Rakim's people came running in to tell us.

"We're done but what's up?"

"Raphael said, the captain got the message and sending officers here." Each of us hauled ass downstairs.

"Is the house done?" I referred to the gasoline they poured around it.

"Yea. Let's go." We ran out and someone pulled up in the car we drove in. All of us hopped in and I'll be damned.

"How you get here?"

"My sister made me follow y'all in case you needed assistance. I was in one of the other trucks." I laughed thinking about Mari sending Rakim. If only she knew how dangerous I really was.

"She's still under the assumption you're the uppity Spanish guy she met." He shrugged his shoulders. The cops

242

were flying by but it didn't matter because the house was engulfed in flames.

****

"I'll see y'all at the wedding in a couple of weeks." I told the guys when they stopped in front of my house.

"Damn we can't come in?" Raul joked.

"Hell no because if I'm not mistaken, my fiancé has something special planned for me." I smirked, opened the door and hit them with the peace sign.

"Whatever." Rakim sucked his teeth and sped out. We'll never be best friends but at least we're cordial at this point.

I went in the house, dropped my keys, stripped outta my fire smelling clothes and went to the kitchen and tossed them in the trash. I made sure the door was locked and walked up the steps butt ass naked, thinking my woman would be awake and down to shower with me.

Unfortunately, she was knocked out. I smiled and moved passed her quietly to shower. The whole time I was in there, I thought about Mari becoming my wife and having my

243

seed. We didn't have a hard relationship at all but there was always an obstacle when it came to the two bitches I fucked with. Had I known they'd turn into stalkers I never would've messed with them.

I washed my hair, showered, stepped out and brushed my teeth. It felt good to have peace in my life. I was even happier no one would bother Mari anymore. I don't know what I would've done if she miscarried.

I shut the light off and went in the room preparing myself for a good night's sleep but canceled it when my woman tossed those covers back and revealed her naked body. My dick woke right up.

"You said I could have what I want when you got home." I tossed my towel on the ground and went straight to her.

"I sure did and I'm about to give it to you." Our lips met and for the rest of the night we gave each other enough pleasure to last a lifetime. Hell yea, I picked the perfect woman to spend the rest of my life with.

Efrain

"Is everything in place?" I sat in Rakim's office listening to him prepare for me to get the niggas back who violated me.

"Yea and the big buff dudes you told us to get are there and ready. Yo, I'd hate to be in their position right now." Ced said and I put my head down. I was happy to know they're about to get the exact same treatment I received.

"A'ight. Did my brothers get there?" I looked at him.

"What? They wanted to be there." He shrugged his shoulders and grabbed the keys. I had no idea there would an audience.

"Can we get this over with?" I walked to the door and stopped.

"I can just let Ced shoot them, if you don't wanna go through with it."

"No, I want to." Rakim patted my shoulder and locked his office door on the way out. I sat in the car and stared out the window.

It took all these years to get past what those motherfuckers did and now I'm about to get each one of them. I almost missed out on getting Gavin because Rakim wanted to kill him the night they found him. He was hiding out with his father in New York. Evidently, he heard my brother had a bounty on his head and fled. When you have so many people working for you, someone will always find what they're looking for.

He pulled up to a spot and I couldn't help but notice a bunch of different vehicles. I glanced at Rakim, who once again shrugged his shoulders. What the hell did he have planned? Instead of asking, I opened the door and smiled as Geri hopped out her car and came towards me. She knew I was seeking revenge but I didn't expect to see her until later.

"Don't be mad Efrain. I wanted to make sure you didn't back out or needed reassurance that you're doing the right thing." I stared at her. How is this woman a doctor and about to go against everything to make sure I'm good? I'm not upset but I also don't want her losing anything behind me.

"I'm good Geri. You shouldn't be here." She took my hand in hers.

"I'm exactly where I should be. Shall we?" I stopped her from walking and planted a kiss on those sexy lips of hers I loved. No, we're not in love but I'm too old to be saying the lips I like.

We walked in and to say I was shocked is an understatement. Mari was sitting on Jose's lap. Jocelyn was standing against the wall speaking to Rakim. Genesis was laughing at whatever Dash whispered in her ear. George stood by the two big buff dudes with Tito and Raul and Levi sat in a chair talking to my pops. The only person missing is my mom and I can guarantee she's probably watching the kids. I knew my brothers were here but not everyone else. Mari waddled over to me. She was due any day now and Jose couldn't wait and neither could my mom.

"We're all here to support you Efrain so don't you dare get mad." Geri squeezed my hand.

"Actually, I'm not."

"You're not?"

"No and I wanna say thank you for being here. It took a lot for me to even speak on what happened. It's only right y'all witness them dying for hurting your brother."

"Exactly! I love you brother." She kissed my cheek and went over to Jose.

"You ready? Hi Geri." Jocelyn asked and gave me a hug. I've been seeing her a lot because Rakim had me coming over to verify each person they picked up. I don't even know if all of them were right but they must be if they're here.

"Yea. I want it to be over."

"It will be." She too kissed my cheek.

"Ugh Efrain. Come here for a second." George shouted and waved me to him. I had Geri go to Mari and went to see what he wanted.

"This is Donnell and Spike. They'll be the ones interacting with our friends in the back."

"Are you sure about this?" I asked. These men were huge like bouncers and about to let us see them do some crazy shit.

"Man, we're porn stars. We always have an audience." One said.

"And the money is worth it." I turned to look at my family. They all stared at my father. I had no idea he paid them to do this.

"Ok then."

"It's time." Rakim sent the guys to the back and told everyone to sit.

"Did I miss it?" Ced barged in with his girl and locked the door. She gave me a hug and told me it's about time. It's no secret him and Rakim were close and she knew. I also know, no one in this room would ever speak a word of this.

"Shut the lights off." I took a seat next to Geri.

Music began playing and the screen came down. It was crazy how my brother had this set up as if we were at the movies but I'm here for it. I think everyone else was too because no one was talking.

"What's up y'all?" Raul was in the video laughing. He zoomed in on everyone and yelled out to ask if the camera had a good view. Rakim told him yes and a few seconds later he stepped out.

It wasn't until he sat that we all noticed the guys naked and handcuffed together. You could see Nicole tied to a chair against the wall. Her eyes were duct taped open so she couldn't close them. My idea. I wanted her to see everything. You could see her tryna blink and the tears streaming down her face.

"Damn. You sexy as hell." One of the bouncers walked in the room and stood in front of Bobby. He stroked his dick and the other one came over and did the same. All my brothers and the other guys had their heads down, while my sister and the rest of the women stared.

"He's pretty big." The women all agreed.

"Genesis don't make me fuck you up in here." Dash shouted and tried covering her eyes. We all started laughing and glanced back at the screen.

"Get the fuck outta here." I give it to Bobby for tryna be tough but dude didn't care.

"I ain't going nowhere. Suck this big ass dick." He rammed himself in Bobby's mouth and dared him to bite him. I didn't have to perform on them but they did it to me so this is what they get. The men got up and stepped outside while the women and George stayed in and stood by me.

"You sucking the hell outta my dick for someone who's against it." The dude went harder in his mouth and all of a sudden Bobby started gagging. The dude pulled out and nutted on his face.

"You ready for this?" He flipped Bobby over, which made the others do the same since they're attached.

"Just kill me please." Bobby whined and so did the others. Dude laughed as he put a condom on.

"No need." And just like that, he forcefully entered Bobby and he screamed out loud as hell. It didn't take long to see blood seep out and I had no remorse. Both guys began giving them the same treatment I got.

"Are you ok?" My sister asked and wiped the few tears rolling down my face.

"I am now." I turned to hug her and she squeezed me really tight. I moved away and she had tears running down her face.

"It's ok Mari. I'm fine." She smacked me on the arm.

"I'm not crying for that fool. My water broke."

"OH MY GOD!" All the women and George started screaming and jumping up and down. The men barged back in thinking something was wrong but not Jose. It's like he knew.

"I bust that ass this morning and now my baby ready." All of us sucked our teeth as he lifted her and carried her outside. Mari was tiny and big belly or not, he lifted her with ease.

"I'm coming Mari." Jocelyn yelled out.

"Go ahead y'all. He can finish the last one." Rakim said.

"She'll be in labor for a while. We wanna see Efrain finish." Genesis stood next to me and put the metal bat in my hand. Gavin was brought out with his hands tied up.

"You always wanted to be a boss right Gavin." I walked up on him and he was crying like a bitch.

"I wonder where these tears were when you almost killed me."

BAM! I swung hard at his head and his body hit the ground.

"Or when you dangled that fucking video over me."

BAM! I swung again.

"You knew what those niggas did in your house and let it go down." I swung over and over. Blood and brain splatter was everywhere.

By the time I finished his face was mangled and some of his body parts were hanging off. I turned around and each person had a grin on their face. Most would've thought it was disgusting but when you have a family like mine, you can expect the unexpected.

"I'm proud if you son." He walked over to me.

"I would hug you but the blood will get on my clothes and your spoiled sister already had Jose call in the car asking where was I." All of us started laughing because we knew she would.

"Here." Rakim handed me a gun and led me in the room where Bobby and the other guys were. They weren't dead but fucked up pretty bad. After the dudes did their thing, they beat the shit outta them.

"Efrain please. I get it." Nicole spoke and I could see how red her eyes were. I wasted no time and shot her in between them.

"All of you will burn in hell." Each one of their bodies dropped when the bullet hit, and it was at that moment when I finally felt free. The weight I held all these years was gone. I fell to the ground and let out a loud scream. I no longer have to look over my shoulder or be paranoid someone will see the video. No one said a word and I'm glad because this was my moment and I needed it.

I sat there for about an hour staring at each body. Geri came in with new clothes for me to put on and some wipes to clean the blood off my face. Everyone but Dash, Levi and Rakim stayed behind to wait for me. I walked out and they all hugged me. I should've told them a long time ago and I'll always regret that but I can't cry over spilled milk. The worst part is over and I still have a lot of healing to do but I'm ok now.

"I love y'all."

"We love you too and happy its finally over. Geri, take good care of him." Dash told her and she nodded.

"You ready?" She grabbed my hand and walked to the car with me. As we sat, a van pulled up with two guys in it. They spoke to Rakim and went inside. It's probably to get rid of the bodies. I called my mother and she cried over the phone. She was happy Mari was giving birth and happy I could finally have peace. Shit, so am I.

Demaris

"Push Mari." Jose held my hand and kept peeking below to see if our baby was coming out. We still had no idea what we were having.

After Efrain handled his business and my water broke, my fiancé carried me to the truck and rushed me to the hospital. I had him call my dad because I wanted him there too. I knew he wouldn't come in the room but I still had to have him in the vicinity. I will always be a daddy's girl and me having a child of my own won't change a thing.

Jocelyn went to pick my mom up with George and Genesis because she had the kids. They all showed up and are waiting for me to deliver. I've been here two hours and couldn't wait to see my baby.

"I can see the head Mrs. Davis." Yea, I was still unmarried.

"Shit, Mari. Our baby has a lotta hair." He peeked and I heard him say hello to my mom who just stepped in. She went out to tell everyone I was pushing.

"How are you honey?" She pushed my hair back.

256

"Trying to push this big head baby out." I felt Jose squeeze my hand.

"Don't talk about my baby." If you're wondering why I'm not screaming the way Jocelyn did is because I received the epidural. Thankfully, I didn't start feeling the contractions until I got here. There was a ton of pressure though but I didn't feel the pain.

"One more push." The doctor said and I felt pressure. I squeezed Jose's hand, put my chin to my chest and pushed hard as I could.

WAA! WAA! I heard and let my head hit the pillow.

"Congratulations on your baby girl."

"A girl? Oh my God! Our first granddaughter." My mom was ecstatic.

"You ok Mari." My eyes started to close.

"Yea. I'm tired."

"Is she ok doc?" He glanced up at the machines.

"Yes, her vitals are fine. She's probably very tired from pushing."

"I thought she couldn't feel it." He asked.

257

"It's not as much pain as a woman who didn't receive one but her body will be just as weak." He turned to look at me.

"I'm fine baby. I just need to rest." He kissed my lips and the baby started crying.

"YO! What the fuck you doing with my daughter?" I chuckled a little because he's already bugging and she's only a few minutes old.

"Sir, I was doing her hand and footprints. I wiped her feet and the wipe must be too cold."

"Yea a'ight. Hurry up and finish. I want my daughter to meet her mother before she goes to sleep." My mom kept telling me how pretty she was and I tried my hardest to wait.

"Here you go daddy." He brought her straight to me.

"Isabella meet your mommy." I smiled when he called her by his mom's name. It was my idea to name her after his mom. He asked me a thousand times if I were sure because he didn't want me to feel pressured. I kissed her forehead and told him to let me sleep for a half hour.

"I love you Mari and I'll be right here when you wake up." I felt him peck my lips again and went straight to sleep.

258

****

"Do you Demaris Davis, take Jose Alvarado to be your lawfully wedded husband?" The reverend finished asking me if I wanted to marry him. It's been three days since I had my daughter and I wanted to be his wife. The ceremony I had planned is next month and we're still having it.

"I do." We stood in front of everyone at my parents' house and finished becoming Mr. and Mrs. Alvarado. I did want to be married before my daughter, however; I knew it wouldn't be possible with how big my stomach was. The dress wouldn't fit.

"I'm sorry you didn't have my last name before our daughter came." Jose moved me up a little and sat behind me in the lawn chair on the back porch. I was still sore and just came out to breastfeed in peace.

"It's ok babe. As long as we're married, nothing matters."

"At least we'll be married before the next one." I didn't bother turning around. He and I discussed having kids close in age and if it meant back to back, oh well. He's my husband and the faster we push them out, the more time we'll get to grow with them.

"Are you ok with the move?" I asked about him moving in with me. Him and Jocelyn lived together for years and now with both of them in relationships, neither stayed in the house. They put it on the market and people put bids in for it already. They are going to split the money.

I asked him to keep the house in the woods and change the locks. Its secluded and very private. He and I, have done so many nasty things over there, I wanted to keep that as our safe haven. Jocelyn didn't really care for it because she said it's a good and bad memory for her and my brother. When I asked her what, she said its where they first had sex but it carried bad memories because he was still sleeping with the chick that gave him something.

"I'm fine. Wherever my wife and kids are, is where I'm gonna be anyway." He kissed my neck and took my daughter to burp her. I fixed my clothes just as my father stepped out.

"Thanks for taking good care of my daughter Jose." We both looked at him.

"What's wrong daddy? You're not dying, are you?"

"Girl move. I'm just thanking him because I saw how bad the other nigga hurt you and I see how happy you are with him. Welcome to the family son." He stood and embraced Jose.

"Thanks." He took my daughter out his hand and walked in the house.

"Yo, your pops ain't shit."

"Why?"

"You didn't see that shit." I had a grin on my face because I knew exactly what he was talking about.

"How he come out here to thank me, then steal my daughter right out my arms? Who does that?" I wrapped my arms around his waist.

"Your father in law. Don't be mad babe. You know she's the first girl."

"Yea but damn. I barely get to hold her when everyone is around." I laughed at him getting upset.

"Don't worry. You can do more than hold me in a few weeks and trust, I'll be waiting." I unbuckled his jeans, and slid my hands in. He pushed me gently against the wall.

"Did I ever mention how you play too damn much." We started kissing.

"I have to please my husband at all times." He stared at me and smiled.

"You got that shit right, Mrs. Alvaradooooooo. Oh fuck Mari." He moaned and not even a few minutes later did he release in my hand. I stuck my fingers in my mouth and he reached over to get some baby wipes off the table.

"I love you ma."

"I love you too babe." We went inside and everyone was talking, eating and playing with the kids. My father still had my daughter in his arms. I glanced around and smiled. This is my family and even though Tito, Raul and Juan recently started to come around, we consider them family too.

"A happy wife, means a happy life right ma." He had his arms around my waist.

"Yup. You know it." We kissed and joined the family. This is the life.

Epilogue

Two years later...

Jose and I, had the bigger ceremony a few months later. I pushed it back because for one... we were already married and two... I had more time to put it together the way I wanted. It was cute and both of us she'd tears as we said our vows. He was madly in love with me and I felt the same.

We welcomed a son, eleven months later and already working on baby number 3. The two of us never could keep our hands off each other. My father told me to start playing hard to get. I think we're way past that.

Jocelyn and Rakim were married last month. My nephew was a mess throughout the service. He only wanted my mom or his mother to hold him. Rakim told her, when his daughter comes she better not even think about spoiling her. Yup, he got her pregnant again too. When you're married who cares how many times you get pregnant. As long as you can take care of your kids it shouldn't matter.

Dashier and Genesis went to the courthouse and he allowed her to legally adopt Kingston. None of us were surprised because she's been around him his entire life. Now they have a daughter and my brother is ecstatic to have witnessed the pregnancy. She did have a few scares of miscarrying but it came from her stressing over the fact of her passing the two-month mark. My mom had to sit down and threaten her about what she'd do if a miscarriage did happen. It was more or less to make her stop worrying. Say what you want but it worked. They're working on another kid after they return from Jamaica.

Levi and George adopted a set of twins and I'm sure y'all know George is a mess. They had one of each and he spoiled both of them rotten. They were turning two next month and you would think it was a wedding or something. I mean George was going all out with ordering animals, clowns and a bunch of other shit. Levi doesn't say much because it's always been about keeping George happy. My mom gets in his ass a lot as if he came from her womb. I absolutely love them together and so does my parents.

Last but not least, Efrain no longer attends therapy and I guess he wouldn't being his wife is the therapist. Therefore; any therapy he may need can be done in the house. Yup! He married her a year later. I asked if it was because she got him to open up and he said, it was that and a whole lot more. She appeared to be in love with him too. I would think she was after watching him deal with the people who hurt him.

They are expecting their first child in a few months and he's a nervous wreck. He is around all of our kids all the time but he always says he can send them home. With his own, he can't. Geri is ecstatic and so is her family. Unfortunately, like most women she suffered a bad heartbreak as well and Efrain was the first person she's been with. They feel the same as us and that's the two of them bringing out the best in each other. We weren't sure Efrain would find a good woman but she came at just the right time like the rest of our spouses.

The End!!

CPSIA information can be obtained
at www.ICGtesting.com
Printed in the USA
LVHW082129101221
705870LV00014B/429